YORK NOTES

General Editors: Professor A.N. Jeffare
of Stirling) & Professor Suheil Bushrui (
University of Beirut)

George Orwell

NINETEEN EIGHTY-FOUR

Notes by Robert Welch

MA (N.U.I.) PH D (LEEDS)
Professor of English and Head of Department, University of Ulster at Coleraine

 LONGMAN
YORK PRESS

Excerpts from *Nineteen Eighty-Four* by George Orwell are reprinted by kind permission of the estate of the late Sonia Brownell Orwell and Martin Secker & Warburg Ltd; and in the USA by kind permission of Harcourt Brace Jovanovich, Inc., copyright 1949 by Harcourt Brace Jovanovich, Inc., renewed 1977 by Sonia Brownell Orwell.

YORK PRESS
Immeuble Esseily, Place Riad Solh, Beirut.

LONGMAN GROUP UK LIMITED
Longman House, Burnt Mill, Harlow,
Essex CM20 2JE, England
*Associated companies, branches and representatives
throughout the world*

© Librairie du Liban 1983

First published 1983
Reprinted 1989

ISBN 0-582-02289-4

Produced by Longman Group (FE) Ltd.
Printed in Hong Kong

Contents

Part 1: Introduction   *page* 5
  A note on the text   12

Part 2: Summaries   13
  A general summary   13
  Detailed summaries   14

Part 3: Commentary   35
  Purpose   35
  Form   36
  Structure   39
  Language   56

Part 4: Hints for study   59
  Useful quotations   61
  Answering questions   62
  Some questions and answers   63

Part 5: Suggestions for further reading   68

The author of these notes   70

Part 1

Introduction

ERIC ARTHUR BLAIR (George Orwell) was born in 1903 in Motihari, in India. At the time India was part of the British Empire, and Blair's father held a post as agent in the Opium Department of the Indian Civil Service. Blair's paternal grandfather too had been part of the British Raj, and had served in the Indian army. In 1907 the family returned to England and lived at Henley, though the father continued to work in India until he retired in 1912. Knowledge of his family's background in the British administration in India can help us to understand Blair's attitudes to the kind of society into which he found himself born. In changing his name from Eric Blair to George Orwell later on in life, he was moving away quite deliberately from the relatively privileged and fairly pleasant existence the Blairs had enjoyed in helping to administer the Empire. The Blair family was not very wealthy – Orwell later described them ironically as 'lower-upper-middle-class'. They owned no property, had no extensive investments; they were like many middle-class English families of the time, totally dependent on the British Empire for their livelihood and prospects. Members of this class were able to move higher in the social scale in what was, ultimately, a fairly flexible society. For instance, their children could be sent to the public schools, good but expensive, which were traditionally associated with the upper classes. With some difficulty, Blair's parents sent their son to a private preparatory school in Sussex at the age of eight. At the age of thirteen he won a scholarship to Wellington, and soon after another to Eton, the famous public school.

On leaving Eton, Eric Blair joined the Indian Imperial Police. In doing so he was already breaking away from the path most of his school-fellows would take, for Eton often led to either Oxford or Cambridge. Instead, he was drawn to a life of travel and action. He trained in Burma, and served for five years in the police force there. In 1927, while home on leave, he resigned. There were at least two reasons for this: firstly, his life as a policeman in Burma was a distraction from the life he really wanted, which was to be a writer; and secondly, he had come to feel that, as a policeman in Burma, he was supporting a political system in which he could no longer believe. Even as early as this his ideas about writing and his political ideas were closely linked. It was not simply that he wished to break away from British imperialism in India: he wished 'to escape from . . . every form of man's dominion over man', as he said in *The Road to Wigan Pier* (1937), and the social structure out of which he came depended, as he saw it, on just that 'dominion over others' – not just over the Burmese, but over the English working class.* Success in life, in the terms in which his family would understand success, seemed necessarily to involve exploitation of the weak, at home and abroad. So, failure, deliberate failure, turning his back on his family and his inherited ideas and prejudices, seemed the only course open to this serious-minded man. In effect it meant that Eric Blair would somehow have to shed his old identity and take on a new. This is exactly what he tried to do: he tried to change himself from Eric Blair, old Etonian and English colonial policeman, into George Orwell, classless anti-authoritarian. It will be clear then, that Orwell's reasons for taking the name Orwell are much more complicated than those which writers usually have when adopting a pen-name.

He turned his back on English imperialism and on his own inherited values by taking a drastic step. For the six months after his return from Burma he went to live among the poor in the East End of London. For him the English poor were the victims of injustice, playing the same part in England as the Burmese played in Burma. From being a servant of the British Empire he became an explorer of his own country, particularly of its working classes. The life he encountered in the East End was entirely outside his previous experience; the schools he had been to were all boarding schools, so he had been at home only during the holidays, and there he was pro-tected from thinking about the less privileged by being brought up to believe that the working classes were somehow less than human, and, indeed,.that they smelt. 'The lower classes smell' was a phrase, he tells us in *The Road to Wigan Pier,* that he used to hear quite often in his childhood.† So in going to the East End of London he was overcoming a repulsion which he saw as typical of his class, but he was also trying to get rid of his own guilt for feeling in such a way about other human beings. (Guilt about cruel feelings towards others is a major theme in *Nineteen Eighty-Four*.) Did the English middle classes of the earlier part of this century believe that the working classes smelt like animals? It is doubtful if many of them did, but certainly Orwell was brought up to think so. And in thinking so he found it so: he describes how as a child he would watch a great sweaty working man with horrified fascination, and get his 'strong bacon-like reek'.

Having lived in the East End he then went to Paris, where he lived

The Road to Wigan Pier, Penguin Books, Harmondsworth, 1971 reprint, p.130.
†*The Road to Wigan Pier,* p.112.

and worked in a working-class quarter. At the time, he tells us, Paris was full of artists and would-be artists. It was 1928, and the franc was in a bad way, so that well-off foreigners could live a bohemian and artistic life fairly cheaply. But the life that Orwell led was far from bohemian; when he eventually found work, it was as a dish-washer in a Paris hotel. Once again his journey was downward into the life to which he felt he should expose himself, the life of the poverty-stricken, or of those who barely scraped a living.

In 1929 he returned to England, where he lived for a time as a tramp. He described his experiences in Paris and London in his first book *Down and Out in Paris and London* which was published in 1933. In the meantime he had taught, worked in a bookshop, and had done some journalism. *Down and Out in Paris and London* was not a novel; it was a kind of documentary account of a life about which not many of those who would read the book at the time would know very much. And this was the point of it: he wished to bring the English middle classes, of which he was a member, to an understanding of what the life they led and enjoyed was founded upon, the life under their very noses. Here we see two significant aspects of Orwell as a writer: his idea of himself as the exposer of painful truths, which people for various reasons do not wish to look at; and, his idea of himself as a representative of the English moral conscience. (Winston Smith, in *Nineteen Eighty-Four,* is the last European representative of the moral conscience.) His idea of the writer as an exposer of unpleasant truths, and as the moral conscience of the society in which he lives, in an old one, especially in English prose writing; it is the idea of John Bunyan (1628–88), of Daniel Defoe (1660–1731), of Jonathan Swift (1667–1745), of George Crabbe (1754–1832) and Thomas Carlyle (1795–1881). It is possible to see these two aspects of Orwell's writing combined in *Nineteen Eighty-Four.*

His next book was a novel, *Burmese Days* (1934), based on his experiences in the colonial service. This was followed by two more novels, *A Clergyman's Daughter* (1935) and *Keep the Aspidistra Flying* (1936). He opened a village shop in Wallington, Hertfordshire, in 1936, where he did business in the mornings, and wrote in the afternoons. The same year he married Eileen O'Shaughnessy. In that year also, he received a commission from the Left Book Club to examine the conditions of the poor and unemployed. This resulted in *The Road to Wigan Pier.* His inquiry was neither a theoretical nor a philosophical one. It did not explain the condition of the working class in England by means of economic or historical theories: it was an enquiry conducted along the same lines as Orwell's earlier journeys among the poor. He went to live among the people about whom he was to write his book. Once again it was a journey away from the comparative comfort of the middle-class life, in order to experience the life about which he was to write. He was an observer, keeping as fair-minded as possible about what he saw, remaining responsible to the objective truth. His account of mining communities in the north of England in this book is full of detail, and conveys to the reader what it is like to go down a mine.

Orwell always put great faith in objective truth. The freedom which he prized above all others was the freedom to exercise normal common sense, to see clearly what was to be seen; the freedom not to be taken in by subtlety and mis-directed intelligence. 'Freedom', Winston Smith writes in his diary in *Nineteen Eighty-Four,* 'is the freedom to say that two plus two makes four. If that is granted, all else follows'.* As a writer Orwell felt it his duty to be the spokesman for objective truth; in order to be serious in the performance of this duty, he was convinced that his prose should be plain and clear. 'Good prose is like a window pane', he wrote in his essay 'Why I Write'.† Prose should allow the reader to see the object or the idea clearly for himself; there should be no muddle or confusion. It was not just that muddle irritated Orwell's aesthetic sense; muddle could be dangerous, because through it a writer might half-convince himself that something had happened which had not. This suspension of the ability to see or remember clearly is the basis of the Party's power in *Nineteen Eighty-Four.* Indeed the Party has devised a mental technique which can be used to control reality, or change the past at will. This technique is known as 'doublethink'. The writer, as Orwell sees him, especially the prose writer, is the guardian of simplicity, objectivity and straightforward fact, and so, in our age, he becomes the protector of the human spirit. In Orwell's mind there is a link between totalitarianism and the failure of simplicity.

If a writer fails to be simple and direct, and lies about what he sees, for whatever reason, his ability to write will dry up. He will become a tired hack if he allows himself not to see clearly. The writer who holds on to the freedom to see things as they are, will, Orwell says, almost inevitably come into conflict with extreme political systems.

It was the writer's duty, then, as Orwell saw it, to keep his eyes open, to keep his prose simple and direct, and to try to free himself from prejudice, inherited or political. When the Left Book Club read what he had written about the English class system and

*Nineteen Eighty-Four, Penguin Books, Harmondsworth, 1975 reprint, p.68. All further references are indicated in the text by quoting in brackets the page number of the edition of 1975.

†*The Collected Essays, Journalism and Letters,* I, Penguin Books, Harmondsworth, 1971 reprint, p.30.

English socialism* in *The Road to Wigan Pier* they were not pleased, and when the book was published it contained a preface by Victor Gollancz taking issue with many of Orwell's main points.

The first half of the book vividly describes the conditions of working-class life in the town of Wigan, and this vividness comes from the sense we have of Orwell as a trustworthy guide. This trust is carried over to the second half of the book which is, in fact, an attack on English socialism of his own time. Basing his argument on personal experience and common sense, but mostly on observed fact, Orwell comes to the conclusion that the socialism of his time was mostly unrealistic and irrelevant. Socialists tended to be middle class and had very little idea of how the workers lived or how they thought. Orwell was convinced that class barriers could not be easily set aside. The kind of socialist Orwell makes fun of is the sort who spouts phrases like 'proletarian solidarity', wears sandals, and burbles about 'dialectical materialism', and in so doing has the effect of putting ordinary decent people off, the people for whom Orwell wishes to speak, the people whom, as the book shows, he has taken considerable trouble to get to know. Before socialism can become a real possibility, and not just a theoretical amusement for cranks, the class divisions in English society will have to go, but they will have to go slowly, because they are so deeply ingrained. There is, though, a strong sense in the book that the class differences may not go at all, or may just simply reappear as another form of oppression, a sense that there may be something in human nature which divides society into ruler and ruled. The differences between ruler and ruled are so great as to suggest that they belong to a different order of nature. In the England of *Nineteen Eighty-Four,* Ingsoc (Newspeak for English socialism) has taken over. Although the Party is socialist in name it is just as oppressive as it maintains capitalism has been. There is a huge gap between the rulers (Party members) and the ruled (proles). Indeed the Party does not bother too much about the proles. They are allowed their mean, ignorant lives, while Party members live in comparative comfort. Inequality, Orwell seems to insist, will always re-assert itself. Throughout Orwell's writing there is the admission that there is something desperately wrong with human nature, despite the dreams men have of ideal societies, or Utopias. One way of describing *Nineteen Eighty-Four* is to call it an anti-Utopia.

Orwell was asked by the Left Book Club to write *The Road to Wigan Pier* because he was a socialist, but, as will be clear, his socialism was of a very personal, individual kind. In a way his

*Socialism could be defined as the political and economic theory that the wealth of a people should belong to the people, that everyone should be equal and that there should be security for all.

socialism was a continuation into the twentieth century of the Protestant English moral tradition.

Having completed *The Road to Wigan Pier* he went to Spain at the end of 1936, with the idea of writing newspaper articles on the Civil War which had broken out there. The conflict in Spain was between the communist, socialist Republic, and General Franco's Fascist* military rebellion. When he arrived in Barcelona he was astonished at the atmosphere he found there: what had seemed impossible in England seemed a fact of daily life in Spain. Class distinction seemed to have vanished. There was a shortage of everything, but there was equality. Orwell joined in the struggle, by enlisting in the militia of the POUM (*Partido Obrero de Unificación Marxista*), with which the British Independent Labour Party had an association. For the first time in his life socialism seemed a reality, something for which it was worth fighting. And fight he did. He was wounded in the throat. Three and half months later, when he returned to Barcelona, he found it a changed city. No longer a place where the socialist word 'comrade' was really felt to mean something, it was a city 'returning to normal', with the workers no longer 'in the saddle'. Worse, he was to find that the group he was with, the POUM, was now accused of being a Fascist militia, secretly helping Franco. Orwell had to sleep in the open to avoid showing his papers, and eventually managed to escape into France with his wife. His account of his time in Spain was published in *Homage to Catalonia* (1938).

His experiences in Spain left two impressions on Orwell's mind: firstly, they showed him that socialism in action was a human possibility, if only a temporary one. He never forgot the exhilaration of those first days in Barcelona, where a new society seemed possible, where 'comradeship', instead of being just a socialist abuse of language, was a reality. But secondly, the experience of the city returning to normal he saw as a gloomy confirmation of the idea we have met before, that there is something in human nature that seeks violence, conflict, power over others. It will be clear that these two impressions, of hope on the one hand, and of despair on the other, are entirely contradictory. *Nineteen Eighty-Four* is given over, almost exclusively, to the latter. Nevertheless, despite the despair and confusion of his return to Barcelona (there were street fights between different groups of socialists), the overall impression his time in Spain left him with was a hopeful one. At the end, while preparing to leave Spain, he was able to say 'I have seen wonderful things, and at last really believe in socialism'. The ordinary decent people of Spain were capable of uniting to oppose the power that would try to oppress

---

*Fascism, founded by Benito Mussolini in Italy in 1919, could be defined as authoritarian, strongly nationalist, believing in force as a means of getting its way.

them. But as time went on Orwell's view of things was to darken, and an overwhelming sense of the futility of man's efforts to improve his lot was to take over.

When looking at the puzzling question of Orwell's differing attitudes to socialism, it is well to remember that the period in which he was learning his craft as a writer, the 1930s, was the decade when Hitler and Mussolini came to power, the decade of Fascism. Hitler called the Nazi party a Nationalist Socialist party, an example of the abuse and distortion of language for political ends that disgusted Orwell so much. And yet it seemed to Orwell and to many writers of the time, among them Christopher Isherwood (b.1904), Louis MacNeice (1907–63), W.H. Auden (1907–73) and Stephen Spender (b.1909), that some form of socialism, which would protect the individual and his freedom to see things for himself, was the only defence against the advancing Fascist armies. The only trouble was, as Orwell pointed out in *The Road to Wigan Pier,* that socialism itself was inclined to insist on its own way of seeing things, and to insist that the writer should suppress his own view of things when they were in conflict with what the party thought. This for Orwell was the end of a writer as a creative artist, because creativity for him was first and foremost a matter of being able to see things as they are. Because socialism often considered that freedom was a possible danger to the movement, Orwell came to feel that socialism could easily have a kind of Fascism inside it, waiting to spring on the party member who dared to be different. To Orwell the freedom to be different within society was what mattered. It is the main theme of *Nineteen Eighty-Four.*

In 1938 Orwell became ill with tuberculosis and spent the winter in Morocco. While there he wrote his next book, a novel entitled *Coming up for Air,* published in 1939, the year the long-threatened war between England and Germany broke out. Here the enemy was very clearly a Fascist one and Orwell wanted to fight, as he had done in Spain, but was declared unfit. In 1941 he joined the British Broadcasting Corporation as talks producer in the Indian section of the Eastern Service. He served in the Home Guard, a wartime civilian body for local defence. In 1943 he left the BBC to become literary editor of the *Tribune,* and began writing *Animal Farm.* The difficulties of living during wartime, with its shortage of food and other essentials, undoubtedly influenced the atmosphere of underfed gloom that the story has. In 1944 the Orwells adopted a son, but in 1945 his wife died during an operation. Towards the end of the war Orwell went to Europe as a reporter.

Late in 1945 he went to the island of Jura off the Scottish coast, and settled there in 1946. He wrote *Nineteen Eighty-Four* there. This island's climate was unsuitable for someone suffering from

tuberculosis and *Nineteen Eighty-Four* reflects the bleakness of human suffering, the indignity of pain. Indeed Orwell said to John Atkins that the book would not have been so gloomy had he not been so ill.*
Nineteen Eighty-Four was published in 1949. Later that year he married Sonia Brownell. He died in January 1950.

A note on the text

Nineteen Eighty-Four was first published by Martin Secker & Warburg, London, in 1949. It was first published in paperback by Penguin Books, Harmondsworth, in 1954. Since then it has been reprinted in the Penguin edition twenty-six times. The text referred to throughout these notes is that of the second of the 1975 reprints.

*Edward M. Thomas, *Orwell,* Oliver & Boyd, Edinburgh & London, 1965, p.82.

Part 2

Summaries
of NINETEEN EIGHTY-FOUR

A general summary

It is 1984. Winston Smith, a member of the Party, which constitutes fifteen per cent of the population, works in the Ministry of Truth, re-writing the records of the past. He falls in love with a girl, Julia, and they create a private world of warmth in the grey, predictable life of the time. They hire a room in one of the working-class areas of London, and they meet there as often as they can.

Winston feels an affinity with O'Brien, an Inner Party member, who he imagines is a kindred spirit. One day O'Brien mentions a former acquaintance called Syme, who is, strictly speaking, no longer supposed to have ever existed. In so doing O'Brien and Winston become accomplices.

Winston and Julia go round to O'Brien's luxurious flat and declare themselves opposed to the Party. They wish to become part of a secret society they have heard of, the Brotherhood. O'Brien pretends to explain the Brotherhood to them, getting them to swear allegiance to it, against the Party.

A few days later Winston is given *The Book,* which contains a scathing and brilliant analysis of the Party's methods. Winston reads it, with Julia, in their room.

They have been betrayed. The man who rented the room to them, Charrington, is a member of the Thought Police, and O'Brien has set out to trap Winston. And yet, oddly, Winston still feels an affinity with O'Brien, even in the Ministry of Love, where he and Julia are taken separately.

Winston is tortured as part of his 'reintegration', as O'Brien calls it. There are three stages in this: learning, understanding, and acceptance. He learns, through pain, how reality may be controlled; he comes to understand, through pain and through conversation with O'Brien, why the Party works the way it does; lastly, in the dreaded Room 101, he surrenders his inner self to the Party. He accepts.

Winston and Julia have always vowed that they would remain true to each other. In Room 101 they have betrayed that vow. Their spirits are broken. At the end, Winston loves Big Brother, presiding image of Ingsoc, or English socialism.

Detailed summaries

Part one: Chapter 1

It is 4 April 1984. Winston Smith, aged 39, returns home at lunchtime from his work in the Ministry of Truth in London, chief city of Airstrip One, which is what England is now called. Airstrip One is a province of Oceania, one of three great powers, the others being Eurasia and Eastasia. Oceania is always at war with one or the other. It is governed by the dictatorship of the Party. Winston works in the Records Department of the Ministry of Truth, which concerns itself with news, entertainment, and the fine arts. There are three other Ministries: of Peace, which concerns itself with war; of Love, which maintains law and order; and of Plenty, which is responsible for economic affairs.

Winston sits in an alcove of his flat, where he cannot be observed by the telescreens, which are nearly everywhere in 1984, broadcasting and watching. He starts a diary in a beautiful old notebook he has found, an act which, in itself, makes him guilty of thoughtcrime, the worst crime of all, because all individual expression is forbidden.

That morning, in the Ministry, there had been the usual Two Minutes Hate, during which the workers sit in front of a huge telescreen and are driven into hysterical rage at Emmanuel Goldstein, Enemy of the People, abuser of the great protector, Big Brother. Goldstein is a man who tries to undermine everything for which the Party stands. He calls, in his bleating voice, for things like freedom of thought, freedom of the press. The hatred in the audience grows and grows, and it is impossible not to be affected by it.

Goldstein's image fades, to be replaced by the image of Big Brother, calm, reassuring. The three slogans of the Party appear: 'War is Peace'; 'Freedom is Slavery'; 'Ignorance is Strength'. Then the audience starts to shout, mindlessly, the sounds 'B.B.', in an act of self-hypnosis. That morning Winston had caught the eye of O'Brien, an Inner Party man, who had come into the Records Department before the Hate session, at the same time as a beautiful, dark-haired girl. A look of what seems to be understanding passed between Winston and O'Brien during the chant. Winston felt that O'Brien knows of and sympathises with his revulsion at the mindlessness of the Party.

Coming out of the mood of recollection, Winston finds that all over the page of the diary before him he has written the phrase: 'Down with Big Brother'. He knows he has committed thoughtcrime, as it is called in Newspeak, the language of 1984. There is a knock at the door.

NOTES AND GLOSSARY:

pig-iron:	blocks of cast-iron, run off from the smelting furnace
sanguine:	reddish colour
backslider:	someone who falls back into old ways or habits
aureole:	ring
goatee beard:	small, carefully trimmed beard on the chin, resembling a goat's

---

Chapter 2

Mrs Parsons has been knocking on the door. She is a neighbour, who comes to ask him to help to free her blocked sink. Something is always going wrong with the flats where they live. The exhausted Mrs Parsons is the wife of Tom Parsons, an enthusiastic Party member with whom Winston works at the Ministry of Truth.

Winston frees the clogged sink – and is then shouted at by the noisy Parsons children. They call him a Eurasian spy, a traitor. Mrs Parson explains that they are restless today because they will not be able to go to the public hanging, a regular form of public entertainment. Leaving the Parsons' flat, Winston reflects how most parents now live in constant fear of their own children, who are being trained by the Party to watch for and report to the Thought Police any unorthodox behaviour they notice in their parents or anybody else. Winston guesses that Mrs Parsons is already terrified of her own growing children.

Back in his room he tries to resume his diary but thinks again of O'Brien and of a dream he had many years ago which has now become associated with O'Brien. In it he was walking through a dark room and a voice – O'Brien's – said: 'We shall meet in the place where there is no darkness'. He reflects that it does not seem to matter if O'Brien is a friend or an enemy. There is a bond of some kind between them.

In his diary he writes a greeting to some future time when life will not be uniform, miserable and lonely as it is now, even though he knows this greeting will almost certainly never be read. The main thing is to stay sane and to stay alive. He goes to the bathroom and scrubs the ink-stains off his fingers. He puts the diary away, carefully placing a tiny grain of whitish dust on a corner of it, so that he will know if it has been disturbed.

NOTES AND GLOSSARY:

impedimenta:	things that get in the way
partisanship:	sharing the same attitude
mutability:	changeability

Chapter 3

Winston is dreaming of his mother and sister. In his dream they are in the saloon of a sinking ship, looking up at him. In some way his survival depends on their deaths. His mother's death, he feels, was tragic in a way that is no longer possible: tragedy belonged to a time when kinship and loyalty meant something; now there is only fear, hatred, and pain. There is no dignity.

The dream changes, and he is in what he calls the Golden Country, a landscape with full-leaved trees and peaceful streams. Into the landscape comes the dark-haired girl with the red sash he saw with O'Brien in the Records Department. With a single movement she throws off her clothes, as if wiping out Big Brother and the Party in a single gesture. He thinks her action a part of another world (a world where tragedy is possible?), and he wakes up with the word 'Shakespeare' on his lips.

The physical jerks start on the telescreen, and, painfully, Winston goes through them. As he does his mind drifts back to childhood or what he remembers of his childhood. He remembers clattering down an iron staircase to an underground station, holding his father's hand, in what must have been an air-raid. He recalls an old man, stinking of gin, his eyes full of tears, lamenting over the loss of someone dear to him.

Since then the war had been continuous. It was difficult to remember any details, though, because history was entirely in the control of the Party, and history was changed to suit policy whenever necessary. For example, at present Oceania was at war with Eurasia, in alliance with Eastasia, and things had always been so, according to the Party line; yet Winston knew that only four years ago it had been the other way round. This fact was obliterated by the Party propaganda machine. All records were destroyed and new ones made to fit in with the new past. This is called 'reality control', or in Newspeak, the language of the Party, doublethink. Doublethink is to know that something happened, yet at the same time to believe that it did not happen.

These thoughts of Winston's show that his mind is not totally under control, but his reflections are interrupted by a bawl from the woman on the telescreen, leading the physical jerks, screaming that he is not putting enough effort into his exercises.

NOTES AND GLOSSARY:

buggers: a slang word (it originally meant a sodomite) meaning malicious, untrustworthy types

Chapter 4

In this chapter we are shown Winston Smith at his work in the Records Department at the Ministry of Truth. Winston's job is to alter records; once altered, the old facts are thrown into the memory hole, where they are incinerated.

Winston likes his work, and is good at it, especially at the most intricate altering of facts, with nothing to guide him except his own sense of what the Party wants, of the basic tenets of Ingsoc. Newspapers and books are constantly rewritten, in line with the present. For example, Big Brother said in February that there would be no reduction in the chocolate ration, but now, in April, there is a reduction. It is Winston's task to alter the account of Big Brother's pledge and turn it into a warning of shortage. In this way documentary evidence can be supplied for anything the Party wishes to say.

The Records Department is but a small part of the Ministry. The Ministry has charge of all information, news, books and newspapers. They also produce material at a much lower level for the proletariat, or proles, in Newspeak, including newspapers filled with vulgar sensationalism, and pornography sent out in sealed packets. It also houses a vast printing works, where the altered newspapers, books and records are printed and stored, until they need to be changed again, in line with new developments.

Winston's most difficult job of the morning is to change a report in *The Times* for 3 December 1983, of Big Brother's praise for a certain Comrade Withers. Withers is now an 'unperson', in Newspeak, that is, he is dead, most likely executed. Winston's way round this is to invent an alternative speech that day for Big Brother, in which he praises a Comrade Ogilvy, who never existed. He knows how to imitate Big Brother's heavy style to perfection. Thus, in 1984, can fiction alter life. Here we see Orwell's description of the artist as propagandist. This matches his ideas about the relationship between writing and politics.

NOTES AND GLOSSARY:
palimpsest: a parchment or slate used for writing on again, after the previous writing has been erased
proletariat: the lowest class in a society; the working classes

Chapter 5

The morning's work over, it is lunch-time, and in the canteen Winston meets Syme, a philologist specialising in Newspeak. Syme is an orthodox Party man, but he is clever, especially when speaking about his work on the Eleventh Edition of the Newspeak Dictionary. They drink their Victory gin (served in mugs), and eat the pinky-grey stew (served in metal pannikins), then Winston gets Syme to talk about his work.

Syme explains that the philologists working on Newspeak, far from adding new words to the language, destroy hundreds of them every day. They want to cut the language down, to get rid of the wasteful vagueness of useless shades of meaning in the old language, or Oldspeak, as it is called. What need is there for 'bad', when ungood would do just as well, for 'better' when plusgood would be more effective? Syme explains how important Newspeak is for Ingsoc, for the Revolution. Now, thoughtcrime is possible because there are still words to express it, but when the Newspeak philologists have done their work there will be no word to express dissent. The Revolution will be complete. There will be a complete orthodoxy of non-thinking. Though Syme is a complete party man, Winston reflects that he is too clever to survive; he will be vaporised, he feels sure. He frequents the Chestnut Tree Café, a slightly disreputable place, a haunt of artists.

Parsons, Winston's neighbour from Victory Mansions, joins them, giving off a strong stink of stale sweat. He collects a subscription from Winston and goes on to talk, proudly, of his children, how his little girl followed a stranger when she was out on an excursion with the Spies, a children's organisation. She noticed he had unusual shoes, tracked him, and handed him over to the patrols.

There is an announcement from the Ministry of Plenty on the telescreen. The standard of living has risen by twenty per cent over the past year. And yet there are shortages of everything. It is also announced that the chocolate ration is to be raised to twenty grammes a week, whereas yesterday it had been announced that it was to be *reduced* to twenty grammes a week. Doublethink ensures that the contradiction is swallowed. Winston wonders if he is the only one with a memory. He looks around in disgust at the dining room, with its battered tables, dented trays, greasy surfaces, thinking that once things must have been better.

The girl at the table behind, in conversation with a man with a mechanical voice, turns out to be the girl with dark hair, the one he saw with O'Brien, the one who reappeared in his dream. She catches his eye, then looks away, quickly. Is she watching him, he wonders?

NOTES AND GLOSSARY:
philologist: an expert in language
nervous tic: a spasmodic contraction of the muscles of the face caused by tension

Chapter 6

Winston is writing in his diary an account of his meeting a prostitute three years before. Her face was painted, and this attracted him. Only the proles wore paint, Party women never did. He went down to a basement with the woman. Thinking of her he thinks of his estranged wife Katharine. She had been beautiful, but empty, eager to believe anything the Party told her. Worst of all, though, she had no interest in sex, in which she also followed the Party line. The Party did not actually condemn sex, but it did everything it could to make it sordid and disgusting. It was a necessary ordeal in order to produce new Party material. There was even a Junior Anti-Sex League, which campaigned for celibacy and artificial insemination.

He goes on with his diary entry, putting down the sordid details of the encounter with the prostitute. Why, he wonders, is real love almost unthinkable? He recalls how the prostitute lay down, how when he turned up the lamp he saw she was old, fifty at least, with a dark, toothless hole for a mouth. Yet he went on just the same.

NOTES AND GLOSSARY:

artificial insemination: the mechanical introduction of male sperm into the female reproductive system

Chapter 7

If there is hope, Winston writes in his diary, it lies in the proles. The proles form eighty-five per cent of the population of Oceania, but they are left very much to themselves. Party propaganda says that before the Revolution they were kept suppressed by capitalists, but they are now also regarded as natural inferiors to Party members, interested only in drink, sex, and gambling.

Winston has borrowed a children's history book from the Parsons and copies some of it into his diary. It is a simplified version of the time before the Revolution, when the capitalists all wore top hats, when children were flogged with whips if they did not work hard enough. A feeling in his bones tells Winston that all this is not true, but how can he be sure, when nothing can be known for certain? Once, though, he had held in his hands concrete evidence of deliberate falsification.

It had been in 1973. In 1965, Jones, Aaronson, and Rutherford, among the last survivors of the original leaders of the Revolution, had been arrested. In the usual way they disappeared for a year, then were put on trial, when they confessed to all sorts of sabotage. They were pardoned, reinstated, but not long after were arrested again, and executed. During the brief period of their release, Winston had seen them in the Chestnut Tree Café. He remembers how jaded and futile they looked.

In 1973 a half-page torn from *The Times* came through one of his information tubes, which contained a photograph of the three men in New York, in Eastasia, on a certain date. But Winston remembered clearly that they had confessed to being in Eurasia on that date. So the confessions were lies and he held the proof of it. As soon as he could he sent the incriminating scrap of paper down the memory hole.

Were he to produce the scrap of paper now it probably would not even be evidence of the Party's deliberate falsification of the past. History would have been written and re-written so many times that the past as he knew it would bear no resemblance to the records. It was the Party's aim to destroy common sense and the validity of memory. In the end it would even be able to say that two plus two make five. Freedom, Winston writes in the diary in which he feels he is speaking to O'Brien, is the freedom to say that two plus two makes four. This connects with Orwell's idea of the writer as the objective conscience of a society.

NOTES AND GLOSSARY:
frontispiece: an illustration facing the title page of a book

---

Chapter 8

Winston is wandering in the brown streets near what had once been Saint Pancras Station. He has risked not going to the Community Centre in the evening for the second time in three weeks in order to be on his own, though a taste for solitude ('ownlife' in Newspeak) is frowned upon by the Party. There is a rocket bomb, and a group of houses up the street is demolished.

Further on he hears a group of prole men discussing the lottery run by the Ministry of Plenty. He finds himself back near the junk shop where he bought the diary. He sees an old man going into a pub, thinks that he must recollect what life was like before the Revolution, and on impulse decides to follow him and talk to him. This he knows to be dangerous.

Inside, Winston overhears the old man asking for a pint of beer, (a measure long out of use), goes up and buys him a drink. He questions the old man, about the capitalists, about whether he thinks he has more freedom now than before the Revolution, but the old man keeps on going off on irrelevant tangents. Winston concludes that the old man's mind is a heap of useless clutter. He reflects that in time no one will remember what life was once like.

He leaves the pub and goes into the junk shop, which is full of useless lumber. The owner has a faintly respectable air. Winston finds a lump of softly textured glass, with a pink, flower-like piece of coral embedded in it. He thinks it beautiful and buys it. The proprietor, Charrington (though the name over the door is Weeks), takes him upstairs to an old-fashioned, comfortable room, which awakens in Winston a kind of ancient longing for warmth and security. There is no telescreen.

Charrington shows Winston a print of an old church, St Clement Danes, and speaks an old rhyme about it. He leaves the shop in a state of exaltation, even thinking of renting the room upstairs.

Suddenly he is gripped by fear. He sees the dark-haired girl from the Fiction Department coming towards him. He now feels sure she is watching him, whether as an agent of the Thought Police, or as an amateur spy. He thinks of assaulting her with the piece of glass he has bought, but he is too paralysed by fear to do anything.

He goes home and has a drink. He thinks of the treachery of the body, how it always seems to betray one at the moment when one needs it most. He thinks of his own future, how he will certainly be caught, tortured, and eventually executed. He takes a coin out of his pocket and looks at Big Brother's face, wondering what kind of smile is hidden under the dark moustache.

NOTES AND GLOSSARY:

anodyne:	something that soothes, distracts; a drug
convoluted:	intricately formed; coiled
lassitude:	weariness, lazy tiredness

Part two: Chapter 1

On the way to the lavatory one morning Winston once again encounters the girl with the dark hair. Her arm is in a sling. Passing by him, she falls and cries out in pain. Winston helps her up, and finds that she has pressed a piece of paper into his hand. Later, at the earliest opportunity, he opens it and finds that on it is written the startling message: 'I love you'.

For a week he waits his opportunity of speaking with her in the canteen. Life is something of a dream for him during this period. The only distraction lies in work. Eventually he manages to speak to her furtively over lunch one day, and she arranges for them to meet that evening in Victory Square, where it will be crowded, and where their meeting, they hope, will not be noticed.

When he sees her that evening it is not safe to go near her as there are not sufficient people about. Then there is a rush to see a parade of

Eurasian prisoners and they join the press. In the crowd she gives him instructions, with a kind of military precision, about when and where he is to meet her on the following Sunday.

They dare not look at one another, but in the crowd she finds his hand. For ten seconds he feels every contour of her hand, while he gazes straight ahead into the eyes of an aged, beaten, grey-haired prisoner on one of the trucks passing by.

Chapter 2

It is Sunday and Winston is in the country, following the girl's directions. He comes to the footpath about which she told him. The ground all around is thick with bluebells and he stops to pick some for her. She comes up behind him and makes a sign that they should remain silent. She leads the way into a clearing in the wood, surrounded by saplings too slender for any microphones to be hidden among them. Looking at her graceful figure he feels old and tired, ridiculous, and somehow unclean.

They kiss and he learns her name: Julia. She gives him a piece of chocolate she has got illegally, and the melting taste stirs a memory of some offence which he would like to be able to undo, but cannot. Julia tells him she was attracted to him by something in his face which showed he was against the Party. Her speech is vulgar, full of the kind of words Winston only uses mentally, but he finds it exciting.

They walk through the wood to its edge. Looking across the pastureland beyond, Winston recognises his Golden Country, the rural landscape of his dreams. A thrush near them sings profusely, and the song gets mixed up in Winston's mind with the light on the leaves, the beauty all around. He stops thinking and just feels.

They go back to the clearing and there Julia takes off her overall with a single magnificent gesture, as in his dreams. He asks her if she has done this many times and to his delight she tells him she has done it scores of times. Evidence of corruption and abandon always fills him with hope. Perhaps the whole system is rotten and it will one day just simply crumble to pieces. The more men she has had, the more he loves her, he tells her. It is not just him she likes, she likes sex itself.

Later, he looks at her sleeping body and thinks that now even love-making is a political act. It is a blow against the falseness and hypocrisy of the Party.

NOTES AND GLOSSARY:

etiolated:	pale, colourless, due to lack of light
knoll:	a small hill
obeisance:	a gesture showing respect, submission

Chapter 3

Winston and Julia arrange to meet again. Usually they meet in the streets, at a different place every time. They walk one slightly in front of the other, talking in broken sentences. They make love once in the belfry of a church ruined by an atomic bomb thirty years earlier.

Julia tells Winston about herself. She works in Pornosec, a subsection of the Fiction Department, which turns out cheap pornography for the proles. She has always been an athletic, outgoing type, unconcerned about ideas. She simply wishes to evade the Party as much as possible, not to oppose it. Unlike Winston, though, she grasps the real reason for the Party's disapproval of sex. It is not that sex creates a world of its own outside the control of the Party: sexual privation produces hysteria which can be turned into hatred, war-fever, and mindless worship of leaders. Chastity helps to produce political orthodoxy.

Winston knows that in the end he is doomed, that he will be found out. Julia opposes this: she believes that it is possible, through cunning and daring, to evade the Party's control, to create a quiet world within. Winston thinks that they are as good as dead, while she feels that they should live while they can.

NOTES AND GLOSSARY:

belfry: upper chamber in a church where the bells are hung

pornography: literature written to stimulate the sexual instincts

Chapter 4

Winston has rented the room above Charrington's junk shop. He wants a place where he and Julia can be alone, where they can meet and talk without feeling the need to make love every time. He knows that renting the room is foolish, but it is worth it. Winston is sitting in the room, listening to a woman, a prole, singing as she hangs out babies' nappies.

Julia arrives, bringing with her real coffee, white bread, jam, and a tin of milk. She asks him to turn his back. When he turns round again she has made herself up with cheap make-up from some prole shop. Here, in this room, she says, she will be feminine. Winston finds her make-up very alluring.

Later, when they are lying in bed, Julia throws a shoe into the corner. She has seen a rat poke its nose out of the wainscoting under the old engraving of St Clement Danes. Panic seizes Winston, and he is reminded of a nightmare he has had many times, in which he is standing in front of a wall of darkness. On the other side of the wall is something too horrible to be freed. There is also a feeling of self-deception in the dream, because he does know what is behind the wall, if he could somehow bring himself to face it.

The moment of panic passes. Julia makes coffee and they eat the bread and jam.

Chapter 5

Syme the philologist has vanished. The weather is baking hot. Preparations are well under way for the forthcoming Hate week. Rocket bombs land, and there are huge, inexplicable explosions.

Winston and Julia continue to meet, more often than before. He feels more alive, healthier; the varicose ulcer on his leg heals up, leaving only a brown stain on the skin. He puts on weight. The room is their special world, their sanctuary from the brutality of life outside. It is as if they are living inside the lovely paperweight Winston bought from Charrington, the paperweight which now has an honoured place in their room of love.

Julia is convinced that the Party is totally invincible. Rebellion is only possible through acts of private disobedience, or isolated acts of violence. She has none of his obsession with the Party's conversion of lies into truths, the way it controls how and what people think. She is not impressed by the piece of evidence he once had (about Jones, Aaronson and Rutherford being in New York when they were supposed to be in Siberia) which proved deliberate distortion of historical facts by the Party. Winston's preoccupation with the Party's lies explains his fascination with the glass paperweight. That, because there are no words attached to it, has remained unchanged and fixed, solid and beautiful, as the past should be.

However, when he tries to talk to her about the Party's denial of objective reality, she tends to fall asleep. She is not interested, and Winston reflects that the Party thrives on this tendency. The public does not realise the enormity of the lies which it is asked to swallow.

Chapter 6

One day O'Brien speaks to Winston in the Ministry of Truth. He refers, obliquely, to Syme, the philologist, who is now an unperson. In doing this he is committing a small act of thoughtcrime, making Winston and himself into accomplices. O'Brien invites him to his flat to see the new Newspeak Dictionary.

Winston now feels sure that the conspiracy against the Party he had longed to know about – the Brotherhood, as it is called – does exist, and that in the encounter with O'Brien he has come into contact with its outer edge. He knows he has embarked on a course of action which will lead, in one way or another, to the cells of the Ministry of Love. He is doomed.

Chapter 7

This is one of the most powerful chapters in the book. Winston wakes up in the room over the junk shop with his eyes full of tears; he has been dreaming. A memory which has been troubling him, but which he could not or would not fully recollect, has finally broken surface. It seems as if the incident, which happened when he was ten or so, has taken place again inside the soft light of the paperweight, which is the world associated with the past, with memory.

It was the time in his childhood after his father had disappeared, when he and his mother and his two- or three-year-old sister were living – and starving – in a big room. Winston remembers how at meal-times he would beg and shout for more food, even though he knew that he was starving his mother and his sister. Between meals he would even steal from the tiny store of food on the shelf.

One day there is a chocolate ration, a rare event. They have a tiny two-ounce slab between the three of them. Winston demands that he should have all of it. His mother gives him three-quarters of it, and the remainder to his little sister, who all the time has been looking at him with large, mournful eyes. Suddenly he snatches his sister's fragment of chocolate and runs out. His mother, in an impulsive gesture puts her arm around the dying girl. The meaning of the dream for Winston lies in the gesture, its impulse to protect the vulnerable. He never saw them again.

His mother's impulse was, strictly speaking, useless and irrational. But it came from a world of feeling entirely hers. The Party, however, tried to obliterate all feeling, all impulse, and at the same time denied the individual any control over the outside world. He is on the point of telling Julia all of this, when he finds that she is asleep. It occurs to him that the proles still have impulses, that they have remained loyal to one another, that they are human, whereas Party members are not.

Julia wakes up and they vow never to betray how they feel inside for one another. They will stay true to that no matter what happens to them in the torture cells of the Ministry of Love.

NOTES AND GLOSSARY:

impregnable: safe against attack

Chapter 8

Winston and Julia go to O'Brien's flat, which is in the Inner Party district, a place where there is a smell of good food and tobacco. They are admitted by O'Brien's servant, and they pass through impeccably painted corridors. O'Brien continues to work when they are admitted to his richly furnished room. When finished, to their astonishment, he switches off the telescreen.

Winston blurts out why he has come: they want to work against the Party. They believe in the existence of the Brotherhood and that O'Brien is involved with it. Martin, O'Brien's servant, brings in a decanter of real red wine and they drink a toast to Emmanuel Goldstein, leader of the Brotherhood. O'Brien asks them a series of questions about their willingness to commit various atrocities on behalf of the Brotherhood and gets their assent. The only thing they are not prepared to do is to separate. O'Brien explains that the Brotherhood is a totally secret society. No one, not even its members, knows how many are involved.

They must leave separately. Before they do they drink another toast, this time given by Winston, to the past. In a few days Winston will get a copy of *The Book,* Goldstein's book. When he reads that, he will be a full member of the Brotherhood. Julia leaves and Winston prepares to go. O'Brien tells him they may never meet again. Winston says if they do they will meet in the place where there is no darkness, quoting his own dream.

NOTES AND GLOSSARY:
persiflage: banter

Chapter 9

Winston is exhausted. During Hate Week, while he was at a public meeting in one of the great London squares, it was announced that Oceania was at war with Eastasia, not with Eurasia. From then Winston had worked ninety hours in five days, altering the past to fit in with the new present, shifting the war of the past years from one part of the world to another.

During the public meeting someone handed him a briefcase containing *The Book,* Goldstein's book. Now, alone, and in his retreat over the junk shop, he starts to read.

The Book is in three chapters, and he starts with Chapter 3, entitled 'War is Peace',. one of the Party's central slogans. The main points of the analysis are as follows:

(1) In 1984 war is continuous, because it consumes the products of human labour. If general wealth were to increase, then this would destroy privilege, and so make it more difficult to control people's minds and lives. War is the means by which people are kept in hardship, and so are controllable. War, then, is the economic basis for a hierarchical society.

(2) There is also an emotional need to believe in the ultimate victory of Oceania, the establishment of total rule under Big Brother.

(3) Yet none of the three super-states of which the world consists, wishes seriously to threaten any other. By allowing war between them to be continuous they guarantee their own permanance. They prop each other up, like three sheaves of corn. There was a time when war was a safeguard of sanity in that, if a war could be lost, then the ruling class had to have a sense of responsibility towards the populace.

(4) In becoming continuous war has ceased to exist. The continuity of the war guarantees the permanance of the current social order. In other words: *War is Peace.*

Winston stops reading and Julia arrives. He begins to read Chapter 1, 'Ignorance is Strength', aloud to her:

(1) There have always been three main grades of society; the High, the Middle and the Low. No change has ever brought human equality a millimetre nearer. In the nineteenth century there had been ideals of human brotherhood, but by the middle of the twentieth century all the main lines of political thought were authoritarian.

(2) The new High are the bureaucrats, trade-union leaders, sociologists, teachers and professional politicians. They control people's lives through the media, and since the invention of the telescreen all private life has come to an end.

(3) It was always assumed that collectivism (the taking over of wealth and property by the state) would lead to socialism. In the event the wealth now belongs to the new High class, the bureaucrats and administrators. Collectivism has ensured the permanence of economic inequality.

(4) Wealth is not inherited from person to person, but it is kept within the Party's ruling group. The Party is concerned with perpetuating not its blood, but itself.

(5) The masses are given freedom of thought, because they do not think. A Party member is not allowed the slightest deviation of thought, and there is an elaborate mental training to ensure this, a training that can be summarised in the concept of doublethink.

(6) Doublethink is the ability to change one's memory of the past at will, *and* to forget that one has changed it. Doublethink involves holding two contradictory beliefs in the mind at the same time, and an ability to believe both of them. A Party man knows he is controlling his reality, yet he also believes that he is not controlling it. The use of the word doublethink involves doublethink.

(7) The Party revels in deceptions and contradictions, all means of controlling reality: the Ministry of Truth deals with lies, and so on. Only through a condition of controlled insanity, where two plus two do not necessarily make four, can the Party leadership ensure its permanence of inequality. If people started to think thoroughly for themselves it would be the beginning of the end for the present system.

So far *The Book* has analysed *how* the Party works. It has not yet attempted to deal with *why* the Party has arisen. *The Book* goes on to reveal this, but before reading on Winston turns to Julia to find her asleep. He too falls asleep.

When he awakes the sun is shining. He looks down into the yard where a washerwoman he has seen many times before is hanging out clothes and singing. He is filled with a conviction that the future lies with the proles, that out of their loins a race of beings will come to overthrow the greyness of the Party. It is a kind of political vision, an answer to all the misery.

Suddenly reality crashes in. 'We are the dead', he says to Julia as they look down on the prole woman singing below them. Behind them an iron voice repeats the phrase, the picture on the wall falls to bits to reveal a telescreen behind it. Uniformed men thunder into the room. Someone smashes the paperweight on the hearth-stone. Julia is punched violently in the stomach and falls to the floor. She is then carried out. Charrington comes in, but he looks different, younger. Winston realises he is a member of the Thought Police.

NOTES AND GLOSSARY:

gelatinous:	jelly-like
feral:	wild
logistics:	science of moving and supplying troops
ruminant animals:	animals who chew the cud
oligarchy:	state governed by a few persons
collectivism:	theory or practice of control of property and wealth by the state
demographic changes:	changes in the conditions of life of a people
vilifies:	throws scorn upon

Part three: Chapter 1

Winston is in a cell in what he presumes is the Ministry of Love. He is sick with hunger and fear. He must keep absolutely still or a voice will bawl at him from the four telescreens on the porcelain walls. The light is hard and he realises that it is never turned off. This is the place where there is no darkness. He has finally found it.

Parsons is brought in. He has been betrayed by his seven-year-old daughter, who heard him talking in his sleep against Big Brother. Later on there are six prisoners in the cell. A seventh is brought in, who is clearly dying of starvation. His face is skull-like. One of the other prisoners takes pity on him and gives him a hunk of bread. There is a deafening scream from the telescreen. The guards come in and the prisoner who offered the bread is punched fiercely in the face, turning his mouth into a shapeless mass with a black hole in the middle. The starving man is brought out to the dreaded Room 101, after screaming and struggling, even offering his children as sacrifices in his stead.

O'Brien comes in. Winston thinks they must have got him as well, but O'Brien says they got him long ago. He also says that Winston knew it would come to this, in the end. A guard strikes him fiercely with a truncheon on the elbow. He writhes on the floor in agony, thinking that in pain there are no heroes. All one wants is that the pain should stop.

NOTES AND GLOSSARY:

Kipling: Rudyard Kipling (1865–1936), English poet and novelist, born in India

desultorily: in a disconnected manner

Chapter 2

Winston wakes up tied down to a kind of camp bed. He has no idea of time, but since the first blow on the elbow he has been beaten and tortured incessantly, until even the sight of a fist drawn back to strike him was enough to bring forth a stream of confessions. His sole concern during torture was to find out what they wanted him to say as quickly as possible, then say it. O'Brien, he feels, is directing everything. He is the torturer, but he is also, somehow, the friend. Once he had heard him say (whether in a dream or not Winston cannot be sure) that he will make him perfect.

O'Brien is now standing over the camp bed. Winston's flaw, his stain, is that he remembers things which the Party insists have not happened. His aim is to teach Winston the technique of doublethink and he does it by inflicting pain in ever-increasing intensity. He reminds Winston that he wrote in his diary the sentence: 'Freedom is the freedom to say that two plus two makes four'. The Party has the right to say that four can sometimes be five. O'Brien holds up the fingers of his left hand and asks Winston how many there are. Winston sees four, but O'Brien increases the pain, not in order to get Winston to lie (he does that anyway), but to get him actually to see five, and at the height of the pain the fingers blur and there could be any number of them.

O'Brien stops the pain and a feeling of love towards him flows through Winston. He feels an affinity with him even though they may be enemies. They are intimates in some way that goes beyond friendship. (The reader might like to pause to consider what Orwell means by this.) O'Brien tells him that they do not simply want to punish him; they want to cure him completely, to eradicate his fault. They want him truly to love Big Brother.

A heavy apparatus is positioned behind Winston, and two soft pads are fitted to his head. There is a kind of mental explosion and he feels as if a hole has been blown through part of his mind. O'Brien holds his hand up again and this time, for a brief moment, Winston actually sees five. Reality control is possible.

At the end of the session Winston asks O'Brien what is in Room 101. O'Brien replies that everyone knows what is there.

NOTES AND GLOSSARY:

hypodermic syringe: needle and cylindrical tube used for injecting drugs under the skin

stratosphere: one of the layers of the atmosphere around the earth

ampoule: small vessel of sealed glass used to contain materials for injection

Chapter 3

There are three stages in Winston's reintegration, O'Brien explains: learning, understanding, and acceptance. He has learned how the Party operates; he must now begin to understand *why* it does so. He must learn the answer to the question he had asked in his diary, and which *The Book* was getting to when he stopped reading. O'Brien asks him what he thinks about why the Party rules.

Winston thinks it rules for the general good, because it under-stands men are frail and cowardly, lacking truth or honesty, so they must be protected from themselves. At this O'Brien turns the dial up on the pain machine as punishment for Winston's stupidity. The real answer, O'Brien explains, is power. The Party rules not for the general good, but in order to maintain control over everyone and everything. The object of persecution is persecution. The solitary human being is always defeated; only the Party survives. The human being can only survive in and through the Party. Through it he becomes immortal. Individual life does not matter; only devotion to the Party does. So completely does the Party control reality that it remakes the laws of nature. The image O'Brien gives of the future is that of a boot stamping on a human face – for ever.

Winston protests, vaguely. There is something, he contends, in human nature that will not allow this to be so, what he can only feebly call 'the spirit of Man'. But O'Brien points out he is the last such man; Winston's kind, the humanists, are extinct. He is the last guardian of the human spirit. O'Brien gets him to look at himself in the mirror, and Winston is horrified at what he sees. The unknown time of torture and beatings has changed him into a shapeless, battered wreck. He is partially bald, and the varicose ulcer on his leg is an inflamed mass of flaking skin. His flesh is rotting. O'Brien pulls out one of his teeth by hand. This is what the last humanist looks like. Winston collapses on to a stool and weeps uncontrollably.

O'Brien points out that he has brought himself to this state. The only degradation he has not been through is that he has not betrayed Julia inside himself. He will have said anything under torture, but inside he has remained true to her.

NOTES AND GLOSSARY:
solipsism: the idea that the only object of certainty is one's own existence
malleable: capable of being beaten into different shapes
vitriol: concentrated sulphuric acid

Chapter 4

Winston is much better. For some time he has not been tortured, he has been fed quite well and allowed to wash. He is putting on weight and even begins to take some exercise. His cell is a little more comfortable than the ones he has been in. He dreams a lot, especially of what he has called his Golden Country, and of Julia. There is a slate in the cell and on it he writes 'Freedom is Slavery', 'Two and two makes five', and, lastly 'God is Power'. He realises that he has accepted. Power is all that matters. Oceania has always been at war with Eastasia; he never saw the photograph of Jones, Aaronson and Rutherford that disproved their guilt. He has given in. Even gravity could be nonsense. O'Brien has said that he could float if he wanted. Winston deduces that this will be so if O'Brien *thinks* he floats and if he, Winston, *thinks* he sees him floating at the same time. But he cannot suppress the thought that this is hallucination, not reality. According to doublethink he should not have any difficulty. When dangerous thoughts enter the mind, thinking should cease. He is not perfect yet.

He thinks of Julia. He feels somehow that she is inside him. Without thinking he cries her name. He realises that while his mind has surrendered to O'Brien he had hoped to keep his innermost self inviolate. In there he hoped he could continue to hate.

O'Brien comes in. He knows that Winston has thoughts of deceiving him. He asks him what his true feelings are towards Big Brother, and Winston admits he hates him. O'Brien says the time has come for the last step in his reintegration, acceptance. Winston is taken to Room 101.

Chapter 5

Room 101 is bigger than the other cells he has been in, and he senses that it is located deep in the bowels of the Ministry of Love. O'Brien tells him that the thing which is in Room 101 is the worst thing in the world. For some it is burial alive, or death by fire; for others it is something quite trivial.

Winston's ultimate horror is revealed. It is a cage containing two rats, with a fixture like a fencing mask attached, into which the face of the victim is strapped. A lever then opens a hinged wire door so the rats can get at the face. This, explains O'Brien, is what lay behind the wall of blackness in Winston's dreams; this is the secret that he knew but could not face. It is the one thing Winston cannot stand. O'Brien calmly describes the horrors the rats are capable of, how they sometimes burrow through the cheeks and devour the tongue.

O'Brien brings the cage towards him and Winston gets the musty smell of the rats. He screams. The only way to get out of this is to put someone else between him and the horror. He thinks of Julia. 'Do it to Julia', he shouts, in a final betrayal of himself. He hears a click and knows the cage door has been shut. He has saved himself through betraying his deepest attachment.

Chapter 6

Winston is released, and he is sitting musing in the Chestnut Tree Café. He spends a lot of time there drinking Victory Gin. He is fatter, thicker and coarser in body. The bad stink of the gin always reminds him of the smell of the rats, though he never names them, even to himself. He reads *The Times* and plays chess.

These days he has a good job. He is on a sub-committee of a sub-committee, made up of others like himself. They meet only occasionally.

Oceania is at war with Eurasia (as it has always been, according to propaganda), and the war is not going well. Winston is troubled by this. There is to be an important announcement on the telescreen at fifteen-thirty hours.

Waiting for the announcement Winston thinks of Julia. 'They can't get inside you', she had said, but they could. 'What happens to you here is *for ever*', O'Brien had said in the Ministry of Love. And this is true. There is no recovery, no forgetting the betrayal.

He has seen Julia. She, too, has become coarsened in body. They spoke briefly in a park on a freezing winter's day, in a clump of ragged shrubs. (The reader will notice the sharp contrast between the landscape here and that of Winston's imagined Golden Country, the countryside where they first made love.) They had little to say to each other, except to admit that they had each betrayed the other. She admits that in the end you *want* the terror they confront you with to be inflicted on the other. As the poet T.S. Eliot has said, 'After such knowledge, what forgiveness'?

A memory comes to mind, of a happy afternoon spent in childhood with his mother and his little sister playing snakes and ladders. He remembers his sister propped up against a bolster, laughing. He pushes the recollection out of his mind. It is false, he decides. He is troubled by false memories sometimes.

At last the announcement comes. Oceania has staged a brilliant counter-attack on the advancing Eurasian army in Africa. It is a great achievement; total victory is within sight. At last the final healing change takes place in Winston. He sees himself back in the Ministry of Love with everything forgiven. He looks forward to the bullet which they will use to kill him some day in a corridor. He realises how pointless it has been to resist. He has won the victory over himself. He at last loves Big Brother.

NOTES AND GLOSSARY:

cauterized: burnt clean with red-hot iron or boiling oil

sinecure: a job without too many duties attached to it

Appendix: The Principles of Newspeak

This appendix is written in the past tense, and, oddly, affects the whole narrative. It is about Newspeak, the language of Ingsoc, but it describes them both as having happened some time in the past, so that we can assume that by the time this appendix was supposed to have been written Newspeak and Ingsoc had come and gone. The appendix does not say when Ingsoc disappeared; tantalisingly it allows the reader to speculate as to what might have happened. Did the proles finally rebel, overthrow the Party and re-establish Oldspeak? The appendix is written in Oldspeak, and it is the kind of sane, objective account that would have been impossible in the Newspeak it analyses so well. The reader should consider for himself the implications of this appendix, and the way it affects the way we look at the narrative. Does it offer a note of optimism after the terrible pessimism of the end of the story? If so, does it work, or is it just a trick?

The appendix analyses the eleventh and final edition of the Newspeak Dictionary, the one Syme was working towards in the novel. The main intention of Newspeak was to suppress heretical words and by so doing to diminish the range of thought, on the principle that if the words do not exist in which a thought may be expressed, then no thought is possible.

There were, according to the Appendix, three classes of vocabulary, A, B, and C: A consisted of all words in everyday use, B of words constructed for political purposes, and C of scientific and technical terms. The grammar of Newspeak was drastically simplified. There was complete interchangeability of the parts of speech. Any word could be used as a verb, a noun, an adjective or an adverb, by the use of the particles *-ful, -wise, plus-, doubleplus-, un-* and so on. This did away with many words: the word 'well' could be replaced by the word *goodwise*.

Cutting down the number of words was not just simply a matter of utility; it also helped to diminish the range of thought. Indeed there were many words in Newspeak which had for aim the destruction of thought rather than its expression. Words like *democracy, honour, justice* had disappeared, to be taken in under the single word crimethink, which told the Party member all the Party wanted him to know about such ideas. Abbreviations were also widely used to restrict thought.

Euphony, the sound of words, was encouraged, so that the party member might develop a gabbling style of monotonous speech, allowing him to spatter forth orthodox opinions at all times without the need for thought. The word for this in Newspeak was duckspeak.

There was a vast project under way to translate the great writers of the past into Newspeak, thus bringing their work into line with the principles of Ingsoc. When this was completed the originals would be destroyed, sent down the memory holes.

Part 3

Commentary

Purpose

In his essay 'Why I Write', written in 1946 (while at work on *Nineteen Eighty-Four*), Orwell says that his aim as a writer has been to make political writing into an art. He starts to write a book, he says, with 'a sense of injustice':

> I write it because there is some lie that I want to expose, some fact to which I want to draw attention, and my initial concern is to get a hearing.*

Orwell had a very strong moral awareness, an inbuilt detector of fraud and dishonesty in the world of politics. His aim as a writer was to tell the truth, as best he saw it, to show up the lies and contradictions in public attitudes. He saw the writer's role as one of spokesman for the moral conscience of a society, so that for him there was a necessary relationship between art and society. If a writer turned his back on that relationship, Orwell maintained, he ran the danger of political irresponsibility, which for him was the same thing as human irresponsibility. There could be no elaborate garden of art for Orwell, cut off from the tempests of modern political reality. Any beauty that a writer or an artist achieved had to be a beauty arrived at in full awareness of the inhumanity and violence of modern life. A writer should be ready to take that on, face up to it, keep his head, and then make his work of art. Art, in other words, should be tested by the trouble of the real world, and by the evil of human nature.

Behind *Nineteen Eighty-Four* there is 'a sense of injustice', a tormented sense of the way in which political systems can suppress individual thought and emotion, and of man's inhumanity to man. The book's purpose is to expose this oppression, this inhumanity. Orwell is also obsessed with the lie, the fundamental lie, upon which the whole political structure of his imagined England of 1984 depends, and that is the Party's insistence that there is no such thing as objective truth. The Party can change the past at will, and doing this is exactly what Winston's job in the Records Department of the Ministry of Truth entails. There is no such thing, the Party maintains,

The Collected Essays, Journalism and Letters, I. p.28.

as truth, so there is no continuity, and in the end, therefore, no humanity as we know it.

Orwell's purpose, then, may be summarised as follows: he wishes to expose the inhumanity of political oppression, and the kind of lie on which that inhumanity can rest.

His 'initial concern' he has told us, 'is to get a hearing' for what he wishes to say. He could, in theory at least, have written a political analysis of the political tendencies in society in the late 1940s, after the Second World War, and these set down his convictions about the dangers in contemporary political systems. But like many a writer before him, such as Edmund Spenser (1552–99), Jonathan Swift (1667–1745), Rudyard Kipling (1865–1936) and H.G. Wells (1886–1946), Orwell chose to set forth his ideas and feelings in literary form, not just because a narrative framework made those ideas and feelings more convincing to the reader (though that was a consideration), but also because the story allowed him the artistic opportunity of exploring them in living terms, of testing them against character. So to get a better hearing he chose, for his story of political oppression and in-human brutality, the variant of the novel form we know as the 'scientific romance'.*

Form

In the novel before this one, *Animal Farm,* Orwell had turned to the animal fable as a way of combining political purpose with artistic instinct. In *Nineteen Eighty-Four,* his last novel, Orwell turned to the scientific romance as another way of making that combination. The animal fable was associated with the Kipling of the *Just So* stories, whereas the scientific romance was associated with the H.G. Wells of *The Time Machine* (1895), *The Island of Dr Moreau* (1896), or *When The Sleeper Awakes* (1899), and with the French writer Jules Verne (1828–1905) who wrote *Twenty Thousand Leagues Under the Sea* (1870). The scientific romance, as developed by H.G. Wells, has within it a set of conventions which allowed Orwell to put forward his political convictions, and at the same time allowed him the opportunity of exploring the complex psychological development of a central character. This Orwell's political conscience effectively combines with his instincts as a novelist. The political ideas are humanised in the process of Winston Smith's development as the novel evolves. Form and structure depend upon each other.

*See Keith Alldritt, *The Making of George Orwell,* Edward Arnold, London, 1969, Chapter 5, for a discussion of the influence of H.G. Wells's scientific romances on *Nineteen Eighty-Four.* See also Norman and Jeanne MacKenzie, *The Time Traveller,* Weidenfeld & Nicolson, London, 1973, for an account of Wells's scientific romances and their background.

Let us look at the formal aspects of the scientific romance, which so suited Orwell's purposes.

It often places a familiar character, whose assumptions about life and reality most readers would share, in an unfamiliar, even hostile, perhaps terrifying, setting. In *The Island of Dr Moreau*, for instance, the Doctor shares none of the hero's ideals about the sanctity and dignity of human life. To the Doctor, life is expendable, a person's mind something with which he is convinced he has the right to interfere, to bring about more fully rational creatures, – less human, but more rational. In many ways Doctor Moreau looks forward to Orwell's handling of the character of O'Brien in *Nineteen Eighty-Four*. In the scientific romance, the setting (landscape, buildings and general atmosphere), not just the code of values, is disturbing and alarming. Often the central character registers the reader's surprise for him; he sees the great land crabs in *The Time Machine*, expresses his horror to his companions, and the reader shares it in his imagination. It is a simple and effective device. In *Nineteen Eighty-Four*, however, Orwell is more subtle; Winston Smith is not a stranger in the bleak, miserable world of *Nineteen Eighty-Four*, a world of clogged drains, sour coffee, bad gin, grey stew and cigarettes that have to be held carefully, otherwise the loose tobacco will fall out. From the window of his flat he can see the enormous white concrete pyramid of the Ministry of Truth, towering above rotting nineteenth-century houses, held up with great baulks of timber, their roofs patched with corrugated iron. All this is common for Winston Smith; he accepts it without thinking too much about it, though he has a feeling that life must have been better once. That continuous misery is the norm, that Winston feels so little strangeness, makes the atmosphere all the more striking for the reader.

There is a telescreen in every room of every Party member's house, continuously watching for any sign of thoughtcrime (Newspeak for a thought critical of the principles of Ingsoc), and even the slightest facial movement of the wrong sort is enough to give the game away to the constantly alert Thought Police. The fact that Orwell makes Winston a part of all of this, the fact that he is not a time traveller from 1948 (except that his human values belong more to that date than to 1984), makes the reader consider the kind of world Orwell has imagined in *Nineteen Eighty-Four* as a human possibility. Orwell uses the form of the scientific romance, but he handles it in a realistic way, in order to drive home his political point, that a society like the one in *Nineteen Eighty-Four* is a human possibility. If Winston had come out of some elaborate contraption capable of time travel into the brutal world of the novel, then the reader would feel that world as being somewhat remote. Winston Smith is very much part of the society of

1984; indeed the work he does, the continual re-writing of the past, is vital to the Party's survival, and the reason he feels different is because he holds views about human nature entirely contrary to the Party's politics, views which most readers would share. So that through Winston Smith the reader's own assumptions about freedom, justice, individuality, and so on, are being tested against an intolerant political system, one with no regard for tenderness, pity or love.

In the scientific romance writers usually expend a good deal of ingenuity imagining the technology and life of the future, its odd contraptions and strange garments. Orwell set his novel just thirty years on from when he completed it (1984 is 1948 inverted) and so saved himself the trouble of imagining a totally different technology from the one he knew. Indeed the general conditions of city life in 1984 are much as they were in 1948, after the Second World War, with its bomb sites and rationing. Orwell explains the lack of progress by the fact that all technical ingenuity has been channelled into developing, on the one hand, ever more sophisticated techniques of torture, and, on the other, more efficient means of warfare. There has been no progress in the general quality of life, and the Party wants it this way; if people were better housed and better fed, if they were not always thankful even for the smallest luxury, they might start to cause trouble, demanding more out of life, and more from the Party. So, Orwell makes a political point out of the similarity between the general conditions of life in 1948 and in 1984.

Another feature of the scientific romance was that it allowed the writer, while pretending to be creating an imaginary world, to analyse and condemn tendencies in the life of his own time of which he disapproved. H.G. Wells was not only a prophet of progress, he was also a prophet of the doom that he saw awaiting mankind if certain scientific and technological tendencies of his own time were allowed to flourish irresponsibly. Orwell in *Nineteen Eighty-Four* is issuing a similar warning. The novel warns of what may happen if certain political and cultural tendencies are allowed to go unchecked. (The reader might ask himself what these are.) Orwell envisages the worst, so that English society, about which he cares deeply, may take stock of itself. The scientific romance becomes a means of social satire, and we see, once again, how strongly Orwell felt about the relationship between the writer and society.

The scientific romance usually concentrates on the reactions of the hero to the strange life with which he finds he has to deal. This is also true of *Nineteen Eighty-Four,* and Winston's developing reactions to life in Airstrip One (what England has come to be called) form the main interest of the book.

The scientific romance usually supplies a love interest: the hero meets a girl, a kindred spirit, and they share the danger and excitement of the world about them, which is hostile to them and to their love. This is true of *Nineteen Eighty-Four*. Winston meets Julia, in many ways a kindred spirit (though there are significant differences between them), and they create a small world of love inside the blank and lifeless culture that surrounds them. Winston's development as a character, which forms the book's chief interest, depends to a large extent on his growing understanding of himself, and his love affair with Julia stimulates that growth of self-realisation. It makes him a fuller, more complete, in every way a healthier, person.

In the scientific romance the hero often meets another character (sometimes older than himself) midway through the story, who explains how and why things are the way they are in this strange, disturbing world, which the romance has created. This figure is O'Brien in *Nineteen Eighty-Four,* the equivalent, say, of Doctor Moreau in Wells's book. He is a sinister rehandling of the type, because he is expert in winning Winston's confidence, getting him to admit his hatred of the Party by pretending he himself harbours a revulsion towards Big Brother and everything for which he stands. He is Winston's betrayer, but also, to add a further twist of complexity, O'Brien sees himself as Winston's saviour in the last section of the book.

One last feature of the scientific romance that Orwell has transformed out of all recognition is the emphasis on logic and reason in the imaginary scientific worlds of Wells and Jules Verne. There the emphasis is on logic and rationality. Doctor Moreau tampers with people's brains in order to make them more rational. In *Nineteen Eighty-Four* there is also a tampering with brains, but in order to annihilate ordinary logical commonsense. The Party thrives on hysterical emotion (this is why it disapproves of sex: sexual frustration makes people more hysterical, and so more easily controlled) which it encourages in daily Hate Sessions. Further, it wants to erode logical continuity, so that it can do whatever it likes with the past, which it alters at will. It thrives on contradiction and nonsense, as shown in its slogans: War is Peace; Freedom is Slavery; Ignorance is Strength. Winston realises that its basic tenet is $2+2=5$, if need be; or $2+2=3$, if need be. This principle of 'reality control' is called doublethink, and it is the opposite of ordinary logical common sense.

Structure

To describe the structure of a novel, poem, or play, is to describe how it grows and develops. It involves, here, consideration of plot, character and symbolism.

Plot

The plot has three main movements, corresponding with the division of the book into three parts. The first part, the first eight chapters, creates the world of 1984, a totalitarian world where the Party attempts to control everything, even private thought and emotion. It is a bleak world of hoardings and slogans, where Big Brother keeps watch. Solitude is frowned upon, individuality is a crime. Winston finds himself opposed to the drab, inane life all around him, and allows himself to keep a diary, a private and therefore rebellious act. He does this in full knowledge that he will not escape. They will find him out sooner or later. He feels a secret, inexplicable sympathy with a man called O'Brien in the Ministry of Truth.

The second part of the novel deals with the development of his love for Julia, someone with whom he can share his private emotion. For a time they create a small world of feeling for themselves, an alternative to the lifelessness around them. They are betrayed, however. The room they had hired was a trap. O'Brien, whom Winston thought was a rebel like himself, is really a chief inquisitor for the Inner Party.

The third part of the novel deals with Winston's punishment, his torture at the hands of O'Brien. Winston, through pain and the breaking of his spirit, eventually comes to love Big Brother.

As will be clear the plot is very simple: a rebel, a love affair with a like-minded and rather daring girl; the capture; the torture and the horror of the instruments of torture; the capitulation. Apart from Winston, Julia and O'Brien there are no other major characters; there is no attempt to create a picture of a range of social behaviour, and the complex personal interactions therein, all traditional concerns of the novel. Indeed, one of Orwell's points is that life in 1984 has become totally uniform, so the old-fashioned kind of novel, which dealt with the variety of life, would be unthinkable. Winston himself is something of a writer; he writes in the Ministry of Truth redrafting the past, but when he sits down to keep a diary on rich, old-fashioned paper, all that comes out at first is a stream of jumbled recollection. The creative intelligence, individuality, the things which give variety to people and to life, have all but dried up in society. Winston (and to some extent, Julia) is an exception; he alone just retains the individuality which is the novelist's concern. It will be clear that Orwell is making a political and artistic point out of the very narrowness of the plot in *Nineteen Eighty-Four*. Winston is the *only* one worth writing about; all the rest are half-robots already.

In doing this, in having his plot revolve around the inner life of one character, Orwell is very much in line with the practice of the contemporary novel, from the Irish writer Samuel Beckett (*b*.1906) to the Algerian novelist Albert Camus (1913–60), to the American novelist Saul Bellow (*b*.1915). It was just as well that this simple plot structure suited his political and artistic purpose, because Orwell was never very good at handling a complex range of characters convincingly. The single plot allowed him to place his emphasis on the workings of Winston's mind, and so focus on the reaction of the individual to totalitarianism, love, and cruelty.

Character

The development of Winston's character, and our understanding of its development, is the main structural force in the book. His story is the, by now, conventional modern one: that of the hero who is outside society, who finds its values repugnant – save that here the society *is* repugnant, by any normal human standards. The hero is outside that society because he is what most people would regard as fairly normal. He is brought into it at the end, he is made acceptable, but at a terrible human cost.

In Chapter 5 of the first section of the novel we are given a bleak description of lunch in Winston's canteen in the Ministry of Truth. The description, based on works canteens during and immediately after the Second World War, through a sordid realism, creates the depressing atmosphere of life in 1984, the sloppy tables, the bad, smelly food, the unswept floors. Something in Winston revolts against this; there is what is described elsewhere as a 'mute protest in your own bones' (p.62) that life has not always been like this, that there was once a time when it was not a never-ending round of work, bed and food, sleep disturbed by dreams, and physical jerks, the telescreen watching over all:

> Was it not a sign that this was *not* the natural order of things, if one's heart sickened at the discomfort and dirt and scarcity, the interminable winters, the stickiness of one's socks, the lifts that never worked, the cold water, the gritty soap, the cigarettes that came to pieces, the food with its strange evil tastes? Why should one feel it to be intolerable unless one had some kind of ancestral memory that things had once been different? (p.51)

In the novel Winston attempts to recapture some fragments of this ancestral memory, in his love affair with Julia. He tries to come to live in a way that is more natural than is possible given the Party and the general atmosphere of life in 1984. He wants a more complete life, a fuller one, where he can have a proper understanding of himself, of his own past, his own buried memories that come out only in dream and nightmare. That is why he starts his diary, on the old-fashioned paper. He wants to come to understand his own past, his own history, in spite of the fact that this is an act of rebellion against the Party, which only survives through the continual re-adjustment of the past. It is appropriate that the diary should be an old one, its paper thick and creamy, because he is trying to set up a relationship between past values and present conditions. He becomes something of a creative artist, who has the past in his bones, 'mute', and wants to give it tongue. By the time we finish the novel, we realise that Charrington's junk shop where he bought the diary is a trap (a rat-trap, even. Why?), that Charrington himself is a member of the dreaded Thought Police.

From the start, from the very first chapter, Winston knows he is doomed. There is no way he will be able to escape the Thought Police, no way in which he will be able to keep his secret. As it turns out, they have known all the time that he has been having rebellious thoughts, and they set things up to help him to condemn himself: the junk shop where he bought the old diary and where he hires a room for Julia and himself; O'Brien's apparent sympathy towards him. Though he knows they will eventually get him, he presses on, especially after he meets Julia, like a man eager to test his fate.

Seven years before the action of the novel begins, Winston had a dream, in which he was passing through a pitch dark room. A voice spoke softly to him, a voice that was associated in his mind with O'Brien, and said: 'We shall meet in the place where there is no darkness'. They do. The place where there is no darkness is not a light-filled paradise; it is not the Golden Country (as he calls it) of his dreams; it is the Ministry of Love, where the harsh electric lights are never switched off, because there are no windows. All rebellious thought leads to the harsh light of the Ministry of Love. As Winston writes in his diary: 'Thoughtcrime does not entail death: thought-crime *is* death'. To commit thoughtcrime is to choose a life outside the Party's control, and, by definition, there can be no life outside the Party. In time they intend to perfect Newspeak to such an extent that there will be no words for any life outside the Party's control. In the meantime they have to deal with rebels such as Winston in Room 101.

One of his dreams is of a Golden Country, the beautiful, peaceful landscape of European pastoral tradition – sheep grazing quietly on smooth green grass, full-leaved trees, a thrush singing, and fish sleeping coolly in brown pools. It is, as the pastoral dream always has been, a dream of unity, where the mind and the conscience are felt to belong fully to the life around them. This dream is the direct opposite to the reality he has to live through day by day, with its dinginess, its drabness, to say nothing of its cruelty.

Once he and Julia have managed to make contact in the corridors of the Ministry of Truth, she arranges for them to meet in a small wood in the countryside outside London. When she arrives they wander to the edge of the wood and discover what turns out to be nearly his dream landscape. It is 'almost' his Golden Country. A thrush sings overhead:

It was as though it were a kind of liquid stuff that poured all over him and got mixed up with the sunlight that filtered through the leaves. (p.102)

He is drawn into a unity with the place, and can forget, for a moment, that there may be some 'small beetle-like man' listening to the song of the thrush, picked up from a microphone hidden among the leaves.

Winston and Julia achieve a unity themselves soon after this in their love-making, a totally natural thing, through which they create a mutual bond of kinship and understanding directly opposed to the values of the Party.

In the dreams he had about this Golden Country, a girl would come towards him, and, with a single brave gesture, throw off her clothes. He would wake with the word 'Shakespeare' on his lips.

Shakespearean tragedy is a major part of Western culture, and the tragedies are mostly concerned with kinship, caring, understanding, and the value of love. Winston himself reflects that only in a world where love and kinship are seen to matter can tragedy be possible: now there is 'fear, hatred, and pain, but no dignity of emotion, no deep or complex sorrows' (p.28). In his dream, the girl who comes to him, generously giving herself, belongs to a world of feeling care, of kindliness and love. This is why, having dreamt of her, he wakes with 'Shakespeare' on his lips. She brings back, in his dream, all the values for which Shakespeare stands.

Now, before he and Julia make love in the real wood, she takes her clothes off with almost the same gesture as the girl in his dreams ('And, yes! it was almost as in his dream'; p.102), thereby bringing into his life a world of feeling, and of love, and also the certainty of tragedy.

In order that they may see more of each other Winston hires the room over the junk shop where he bought the diary, and a beautiful old paperweight, over a hundred years old, made of rainwater glass. There their love deepens, and they recover something of the feelings of the past, symbolised by the paperweight. This room is a world of love and a world given over to the past; an engraving of an old church hangs on the wall.

As Winston's love for Julia deepens, as his feeling of kinship for her grows, his own recovery of his past improves. With this new love the love his mother had for him and for his young sister comes back

into his mind. And with it come the long-forgotten memories of the
selfish way in which he treated them.

From time to time a certain memory has troubled him. He has never
remembered it clearly, though he nearly did when Julia gave him the
real chocolate to eat when they met for the first time, in the country.
In Chapter 7 of Part two the full recollection comes through in a dream
and Winston wakes with his eyes full of tears. It is as if the whole scene
has taken place again inside the glass paperweight.

He remembers how, after his father had left them, his mother took
care of them, how she would move about the tiny room, and how she
would quieten his baby sister, a tiny, ailing, very silent child of two or
three, with a face made 'simian by thinness' (p.132). He remembers
in his dream how underfed they were, and how he would shout and
scream like an animal for more than his share, even though he knew
that he was starving them. He would grab bits from his sister's
plate.

One day, he remembers, his mother arrived home with a small bar of
chocolate. (This is why the memory nearly broke surface when Julia
gave him the chocolate in the country.) Although it should be divided
into three pieces Winston hears himself in his dream 'demanding in a
loud booming voice' that he be given the lot. His mother breaks it into
two and gives him the larger piece, the smaller to the child. He grabs
hers as well and starts to run off. Then his mother takes the child to her
breast and puts her arm around her:

> Something in the gesture told him that his sister was dying. He
> turned and fled down the stairs, with the chocolate growing sticky in
> his hand. . . . The dream was still vivid in his mind, especially the
> enveloping protecting gesture of the arm in which its whole meaning
> seemed to be contained. (p.134)

His mother's pointless gesture contains the meaning of the dream
because it is a gesture of love. It takes his love for Julia to awaken the
memory of his mother's love for his dying sister. It is the same
protective love which he remembers seeing in the film which he records
in his diary early in the book. There a refugee woman in a boat covered
a little boy with her arm in a useless attempt to protect him from a
hail of bullets from a helicopter. Love, protection, kinship – all these
things are useless, but, Winston comes to understand, they are all that
matter. Loyalty matters, not loyalty to the Party, or to the principles of
Ingsoc, but to one another as human beings. His mother's gesture
stands for this instinctive loyalty. So that while the dream brings to
the surface his own selfishness and violence, it also brings back the
memory of his mother's humanity. The remembrance, even of his own
guilt, is a healing thing. It makes him a fuller human being to

recollect the past. This is why Winston, throughout the novel, is preoccupied with the way the Party wishes to erode the past. He knows that the erosion of the past is the erosion of humanity. If a man cannot face up to his own guilt, if he cannot remember the love of others, then the Party can do all it wishes with him, because he is no longer a full man, no longer capable of feeling.

Winston's love for Julia, then, awakens him to himself; it puts him in touch with his past, his own selfishness, and his mother's generous love. This awakening is a healing thing, as we see when Winston's ulcer on his leg heals up; all that is left is a brown stain on the skin. The reader will see how Winston's obsession with doublethink, the Party's technique for controlling reality, especially the memory of what has happened, relates to Winston's discovery of a fuller humanity through love. Love provokes memory of love, which makes a fuller, more unified man, which brings a dignity back into life, the dignity of living with an understanding of good and evil, the dignity to choose based on past experience. Doublethink gets rid of choice, would even get rid of good and evil altogether. Indeed Newspeak (the language of doublethink) will eventually do away with the word 'evil', and other complicated words, which involve decision and choice. The words not being there, it will be impossible to think dangerous thoughts.

Winston wants to recall his humanity, the good and the bad, and be himself. This he does through love. The reader will see how closely related are the political aspects and the human aspects of this novel. Indeed, at one point Orwell writes that Winston's and Julia's embrace of love (again the enfolding gesture) 'was a blow struck against the Party. It was a political act' (p.104). The reader will also be able to see why it is proper to consider the growth of Winston's character under the general heading of 'Structure'. It is through the explorations of Winston's development that the political ideas and the human elements of the book are drawn together: even the symbols, the Golden Country, for example, and the paperweight, serve to illuminate Winston's understanding of himself. The dream that links past and present takes place inside the paperweight. In this way general and particular, idea and feeling, symbol and emotion, should cohere in an artistic structure that is not just a makeshift ramming together of odds and ends.

The dream reveals the value of love to Winston. He and Julia vow to stay true to that love no matter what happens. They will keep their innermost feelings 'impregnable' (p.132). The rest of the novel tests the value of this vow, and in doing so moves into tragedy.

They are caught. The room, it turns out, is a trap, with hidden microphones, even a telescreen behind the old engraving. They are taken separately to the Ministry of Love.

The last section of the novel, Winston's punishment in the
Ministry of Love, is tragic, in the full sense of that word, because he
has, through love, attained a dignity of humanity, the stature
necessary for tragedy. He has become, through his understanding of
Julia, and of himself, a more complete man, only to be plunged into
the degradations of the Ministry of Love. The sense of pitiful and
terrible waste, always something we find in tragedy, is very strong.
Had Orwell not done his work, had he not shown us the gradual
healing power of love, and Winston's growth into something like
completeness, then the sense of waste would not be there, and the novel
would not be one of the great modern versions of tragedy. Orwell
has given a tragic dimension to the scientific romance.

Winston always knew his attempt at self-realisation would bring
him to the torture chambers of the Ministry of Love. O'Brien, who is to
be his torturer, who is to save him from himself, points this out
soon after he arrives: 'You knew this, Winston', he says; 'don't
deceive yourself. You did know it – you have always known it' (p.192).

There are three stages in what O'Brien calls Winston's 'reintegration', his being washed clean of all rebellious thought; these are
learning, understanding, and acceptance. He first learns that the
Party controls reality, that there is no such thing as objective truth.
That is why history can, indeed must, be changed, because all
individual memory and perception is faulty. He has to unlearn the
very thing that gave him consolation at the beginning of the book:
'stones are hard, water is wet, objects unsupported fall towards the
earth's centre' (p.68). Reality, O'Brien explains, is not something the
individual mind can see for itself, that involves the freedom of
saying two plus two makes four. There are times when the party will
want two plus two to make five, or even three. So the individual
mind, logical continuity, and memory, need to be controlled, and the
way in which they are controlled is doublethink. O'Brien gives him a
practical example of this: he holds out a photograph of the three
traitors, Jones, Aaronson, and Rutherford, the same photograph that
Winston had seen once, which proved to him that the Party does
change the past. O'Brien throws the photograph down a memory hole
and says it never existed:

'But it did exist! It does exist! It exists in memory. I remember it.
You remember it.'
'I do not remember it,' said O'Brien.
　　Winston's heart sank. That was doublethink. He had a feeling of
deadly helplessness. If he could have been certain that O'Brien
was lying, it would not have seemed to matter. But it was perfectly
possible that O'Brien had really forgotten the photograph. And if so,

then already he would have forgotten his denial of remembering it, and forgotten the act of forgetting. How could one be sure that it was simply trickery? Perhaps that lunatic dislocation in the mind could really happen: that was the thought that defeated him. (pp.198–9)

Winston, through love, has learnt that part of the dignity of being human involves consistency, which involves remembering the way things were, so that one can understand why things are. Doublethink makes nonsense of sanity and ordered logic; it makes nonsense of the human mind's capacity for judging on the evidence of its senses. The past can be changed because the human mind can be changed, at the desire of the Party. The Party is collective and immortal. Memory, fact, logic, do not matter by comparison. As the slogan runs: 'Who controls the past controls the future: who controls the present controls the past'.

O'Brien holds up four fingers and tries, by using pain, to get Winston to see five. He does not want him to lie, he wants him actually to be able to see five when he wishes. He fits him up to a machine which blanks out part of Winston's mind, so that he can, for a moment, see five instead of four. Winston has learned that it is possible for reality to be controlled, and for him to see it the Party's way.

The next stage, after learning, is understanding, understanding why the Party exists. Winston, when asked, thinks that the Party rules for the good of the people, that the Party knows how frail and cowardly men are, how incapable of controlling themselves, so they need reality to be controlled for them. O'Brien dismisses this as stupid: the real reason for the Party's existence is power, pure power, nothing else. 'Power is not a means, it is an end'. The image he gives Winston of the future is a totally savage one: 'If you want a picture of the future, imagine a boot stamping on a human face – for ever' (p.215).

Inside him Winston still has the conviction that the Party cannot survive for ever, that the proles, who have not killed off their natural loyalties, will rise up and overthrow it. Winston cannot offer O'Brien any evidence to support this conviction; he simply believes in some principle, some spirit – not God, but the spirit of Man. Winston considers himself a man, but if he is a man, O'Brien says, he is the last man. Then O'Brien puts him through the worst degradation so far. He gets him to take off his clothes and stand in front of a three-sided mirror, so that Winston can see what he has become through an unknown time of pain and torture in 'the place where there is no darkness'. The 'guardian of the human spirit', as O'Brien mockingly calls him, has become a shrivelled, balding, rotting wreck of humanity. The student should read very carefully for himself the description of

Winston as he sees himself in the mirror on p.218. Notice how the ulcer has flared up again; now it is a raw mass of flaking skin. In this passage Orwell has described the condition of the last European humanist. The values of humanism, that gave man a tragic dignity, are gone, according to Orwell. Winston Smith is 'a bag of filth', and O'Brien can pull a tooth out of his rotting gums with his hand. He has understood that he is as nothing in the Party's never satisfied search for power.

The only degradation of spirit he has not been through is the betrayal of Julia. He has, inside himself, remained true to her. O'Brien knows this.

The last stage of his 'conversion' to the Party orthodoxy is acceptance.* He has to accept Big Brother, he has to come to love him, but before that is possible his love for Julia must be 'cauterized out' (p.233). This takes place in Room 101, where he really wants them to put the cage with the stinking rats on her face rather than on his. This is the ultimate degradation, his betrayal of her, and of his vow to her that his feelings for her would not change.

In the last chapter, he is released. He has grown fatter, coarser, and drinks too much in the Chestnut Tree Café. He meets Julia one day, and they talk briefly in a windswept clump of bushes, a pathetic contrast to the Golden Country where they once made love. She too has grown thicker and coarser, and she tells him that she betrayed him in Room 101, just as he betrayed her. All love for her is dead. O'Brien had said to Winston that they would empty him, then fill him up with themselves, and this is what happens at the end. There is an announcement on the telescreen in the Café, about a huge victory in Africa. His soul is 'white as snow', empty, waiting to be filled, and suddenly he realises that it is filling to overflowing with love for Big Brother. The struggle is finished. He has accepted Big Brother. All his misunderstandings were needless self-will. All that remains now is for him to be shot, in the Ministry of Love, in the back of the head, as is the custom.

A good deal of space has been given to the development of Winston's character, through love, and his chastisement in the ironically titled Ministry of Love, because Winston's character is the central interest in the book. Orwell's approach is narrow but effective: he wants to examine how the human spirit might fare under the worst possible conditions, so he does it by showing us the interior life of one man. The human spirit, it may be said, does not fare well in Orwell's imagined totalitarian world.

*The word 'conversion' is Alan Sandison's in *The Last Man in Europe,* Macmillan, London, 1974, p.182.

Here is a summary of the main points made about Winston's character:

(1) Winston has a sense that there was once a time when things were better than they are in 1984, a 'mute feeling in his bones'.

(2) He is concerned with individual freedom and expression. This is why he starts his diary, a personal record. The Party wants to control all records.

(3) His love for Julia expands his world of feeling, almost makes his dreams come true.

(4) It opens up his life for him, so he starts to remember, again something totally opposed to Party policy. It wishes to control the past.

(5) He remembers his mother's love for his sister and his own brutish selfishness. Remembering that guilt and that love he acquires a dignity that makes him capable of tragic sorrow.

(6) He vows to stay true to Julia, not to betray her.

(7) His punishment in the Ministry of Love sets out to erode all the dignity he has acquired. He learns reality control, understands the Party's motive, power, and is broken by the sight of his own wrecked humanity.

(8) In Room 101 he betrays Julia, just as many years before he betrayed his tiny sister.

(9) After his release he accepts Big Brother.

Orwell pays little attention to the other characters in the novel, apart from Julia and O'Brien. Julia is not a complex character. She has a natural, unthinking enjoyment of life and of sex. Winston is fascinated by her understanding of the connection between chastity and Party orthodoxy. Sexual frustration, she maintains, makes people hysterical and they have to be hysterical if they are to be marching up and down all the time, shouting their hatred for Goldstein. In their private world above the junk shop she wears make-up and behaves like 'a woman, not a Party comrade' (p.117). The big difference between Julia and Winston is that she does not share his obsession with the Party's altering of the past. She is not interested in truth, and in the preserving of truth (see their discussion of the photograph of Jones, Aaronson and Rutherford on pp.126–7) but in Winston and herself. In the end she betrays him in Room 101, just as he betrays her. The most significant aspect of her character is how she opens Winston up to a fuller understanding of himself, and she does so by her natural affection and warmth.

O'Brien is more enigmatic. He is a member of the Inner Party and Winston has felt a secret understanding between them for years. He is a large man, with a 'prize-fighter's physique' (p.12), but he also possesses a curious, almost old-fashioned elegance in the fastidious way he resettles his spectacles on his nose: Winston feels that O'Brien is not perfectly orthodox, that like him he has secret rebellious thoughts, so that when their eyes meet during the Hate Session described in Chapter 1 Winston is convinced that O'Brien knows of and sympathises with his attitude.

The voice in Winston's dream that said: 'We shall meet in the place where there is no darkness' is associated with O'Brien. By the end of the novel we know that this place is the Ministry of Truth, and that O'Brien has, over the years, led Winston into the trap of revealing himself. But even in Chapter 2, as Winston recalls the dream, it is made clear that in an odd way it does not seem to matter whether O'Brien is a friend or an enemy: 'There was a link of understanding between them, more important than affection or partisanship' (p.24).

O'Brien, of course, is a totally orthodox Inner Party member, one of the inquisitors in the Ministry of Truth. He gets Winston to come to his flat by mentioning the vanished philologist, Syme, something forbidden by Party policy: those who disappear, for whatever reason, become 'unpersons' – that is, they never existed. Once Winston and Julia are in O'Brien's flat he switches off the telescreen (a privilege which, he explains, Inner Party members have), gives them real wine to drink, and pretends to reveal to them that he belongs to the Brotherhood, a revolutionary organisation with Emmanuel Goldstein as its figurehead, dedicated to the overthrow of Ingsoc. He gets them to swear allegiance to the Brotherhood by making them vow to commit all sorts of atrocities against the Party if it becomes necessary: even to throw sulphuric acid in a child's face. O'Brien promises to get *The Book* to Winston, which reveals the truth about the principles of Ingsoc. Before they leave Winston drinks a toast, typically, to the past.

When they meet again in the Ministry of Love, O'Brien reminds Winston that all along he has known exactly where his thoughts and actions would lead him. O'Brien supervises his torture, but as he explains, the Party does not simply want to reduce an individualist like Winston, who believes in objective truth, to a broken wreck: they also want to change the way he thinks. They want to wash all self out of him, make his soul 'white as snow' (p.239) and then fill him up with the Party, with love for Big Brother.

As Alan Sandison has shown, the religious connotations of Winston's experiences in the Ministry of Love are not accidental.* O'Brien conducts himself like an inquisitor from the Spanish Inquisition, trying to get Winston to renounce his heresies (Orwell has Winston use the word 'heresy' to describe common sense on p.68). Winston's heresy is his insistence on the individual's right to make up his mind on the

*See Alan Sandison, *The Last Man in Europe.*

basis of perceived fact and past experience. This, according to O'Brien, is arrogance. Only the Party, which is 'collective and immortal', can perceive the truth, so that:

> 'Whatever the Party holds to be truth, *is* truth. It is impossible to see reality except by looking through the eyes of the Party. That is the fact that you have got to relearn, Winston. It needs an act of self-destruction, an effort of the will. You must humble yourself before you can become sane'. (p.200)

The religious language here is unmistakable. O'Brien's attitude is very like that of the intolerant Roman Catholic Church of the middle ages, or of the earlier part of this century. His name has indeed even Irish connotations. There is a touch of the Roman Catholic prelate about him, just as there is a touch of the Lutheran Protestant in Winston. Winston insists on the rights of the individual conscience over collective orthodoxy right up to the end. He is an embodiment of the humanist spirit which Orwell saw as being attached to the Protestant stress on the individual, as against the Catholic stress on orthodoxy. O'Brien, though he recalls Catholic torturers of the Inquisition, is also a totally orthodox Party man, believing implicitly in the principles of Ingsoc, Newspeak for English Socialism. As Alan Sandison has shown, Orwell always saw a similarity between socialist totalitarianism and orthodox Catholicism:

> The Catholic and the Communist are alike in assuming that an opponent cannot be both honest and intelligent. Each of them tacitly claims that 'the truth' has already been revealed, and that the heretic, if he is not simply a fool, is secretly aware of 'the truth' and merely resists it out of selfish motives.*

Winston stands for Protestant individualism, bearing witness to the truth of common sense, of normal life, and of human affection, until very near the end.

And yet time and again Orwell makes the point that, in a way, it does not matter whether O'Brien is a friend or an enemy. In the Ministry of Love, even during the torture which is being used to teach him doublethink, a feeling of love for O'Brien overwhelms him:

> He had never loved him so deeply as at this moment, and not merely because he had stopped the pain. The old feeling, that at bottom it did not matter whether O'Brien was a friend or an enemy, had come back. O'Brien was a person who could be talked to. Perhaps one did not want to be loved so much as to be understood. . . .

Inside the Whale and Other Essays, Penguin Books, Harmondsworth, 1976 reprint, p.162.

In some sense that went deeper than friendship, they were intimates: somewhere or other, although the actual words might never be spoken, there was a place where they could meet and talk. (pp.202–3)

The bond between torturer and victim is a familiar theme in modern writing, especially in the stories of the Czech writer Franz Kafka (1883–1924): here, Winston has this curious feeling of intimacy with O'Brien because through O'Brien the worst possible truth about human nature is revealed. There is a satisfaction in having our fears confirmed, a relief in finding out that what one suspected to be true is true after all. Winston, in the torture chamber of the Ministry of Love, is brought into intimate contact with the cruelty and violence that lie behind the slogans of Ingsoc. O'Brien understands Winston, he is even sympathetic; his task is not so much to punish him as to convert him.

There is also a sense in which Winston is relieved to be tortured, that he is glad to be found out at last. Before he met Julia he had strong moods of self-disgust and part of the action of love on his spirit is to make him remember his own cruelty and violence as a child. He feels, in a way, that he deserves the pain of torture, and that by inflicting it O'Brien becomes his saviour. There is a mood of 'We are arrant knaves all' (a phrase from Shakespeare's *Hamlet*) in *Nineteen Eighty-Four*.

Other characters are relatively minor: Parsons is a greasy, enthusiastic Party member who sweats a lot. Winston finds him physically revolting. He ends up in the Ministry of Love too, betrayed by his children who heard him saying 'Down with Big Brother' in his sleep. Children are encouraged to inform on their parents in 1984.

Syme is a philologist working on the Newspeak Dictionary, whom Winston meets at lunch. Winston realises that Syme, though entirely orthodox, is too clever to survive. And in time he disappears, is 'vaporized'. Ampleforth is a poet, who is imprisoned for allowing the word 'God' to remain at the end of a line of a poem by Kipling.

Charrington sells Winston a diary and a paperweight in a junk shop in an out-of-the-way part of London. He rents a room to Winston, encouraging him in his re-creation of a little bit of the past. The junk shop is a trap and Charrington is a member of the Thought Police.

Symbolism

Symbolism is a very effective device in the construction of a novel. Used judiciously, it can draw themes together, illuminate or underline certain features of character or thought. The three main symbols in this novel are: the Golden Country, the paperweight, and the proles.

The Golden Country has been dealt with in discussing the development of Winston's character. It may be useful to summarise the main points about it here.

(1) It is a version of the old European pastoral landscape, which Winston sees in dreams. It is a place of great beauty, peace, and unity, where the observer can be at one with his surroundings.

(2) When Winston and Julia meet alone for the first time he finds that the landscape at the edge of the wood where they make love is almost exactly like the one of his dreams. This is a sign of the fulfilment Julia is to bring.

The paperweight, in its soft beauty, its roundness, with the tiny fragment of coral embedded in it, symbolises that fulfilment. It is associated with the past, with continuity: 'It's a little chunk of history that they've forgotten to alter' (p.119). It has remained constant despite the instability of the past which is the central tenet of Ingsoc. It stands, too, for the small world of love which Winston and Julia create for themselves: indeed when the idea of renting the room over the junk shop first floated into Winston's head it came in the form of 'a vision of the glass paperweight mirrored by the surface of the gateleg table' (p.112). Later on Orwell makes the identification between the room and the paperweight, and between the two lovers and the fragment of coral, quite explicit:

> He turned over towards the light and lay gazing into the glass paperweight. The inexhaustibly interesting thing was not the fragment of coral but the interior of the glass itself. There was such a depth of it, and yet it was almost as transparent as air. It was as though the surface of the glass had been the arch of the sky, enclosing a tiny world with its atmosphere complete. He had the feeling that he could get inside it, and that in fact he was inside it, along with the mahogany bed and the gateleg table, and the clock and the steel engraving and the paperweight itself. The paperweight was the room he was in, and the coral was Julia's life and his own, fixed in a sort of eternity at the heart of the crystal. (p.120)

Later still, when he has the dream which recalls his mother and his young sister, it takes place inside the paperweight: 'the surface of the glass was the dome of the sky, and inside the dome everything was flooded with clear soft light in which one could see into interminable distances' (p.131). Not only has the paperweight remained constant, a little solid 'chunk of history', evidence of a time when such useless things were valued for their beauty, it also works as a symbol of the unity of feeling Winston and Julia have found. Furthermore, because the dream takes place inside it, it stands for the coherence in Winston's own life and history which the dream brings. The dream recalls his mother's love for his sister. It had been:

> . . . comprehended by – indeed, in some sense it had consisted in – a gesture of the arm made by his mother, and made again thirty years later by the Jewish woman he had seen on the news film, trying to shelter the small boy from the bullets. . . . (p.131)

These gestures of the arm are enfolding, protecting gestures, of useless but natural love. Their roundness is connected to the soft roundness of the rainwater glass of the paperweight, itself protecting the tiny pink fragment of coral within. It may be observed that Orwell takes full advantage of the suggestions of circularity in the word 'comprehended' in the above quotation. The circular gesture of enfolding protective love is the gesture of human kinship, pointless loyalty, which the Party has almost driven out of life, but which make possible the dignity of tragedy. When the Thought Police come crashing in, one of them smashes the paperweight on the hearthstone, thereby shattering the small world of feeling Winston and Julia have created:

> The fragment of coral, a tiny crinkle of pink like a sugar rosebud from a cake, rolled across the mat. How small, thought Winston, how small it always was! (p.177)

The proles are the lower classes in 1984 and though they form eighty-five per cent of the population, they have very little importance in the eyes of the Party. They are not much better than slaves, and they are kept in submission through ignorance. A special section in the Ministry of Truth prints pornography for them, and the state-run lotteries also help to keep them amused. The Party does not bother too much about them; they are more or less allowed to go their own way as they are for the most part thoughtless and stupid, without the will or the desire to create trouble.

For Winston, though, they have a symbolic value. 'If there is hope it lies in the proles', he writes in his diary. Only they have the force that could overthrow the Party, and he looks forward to some vague time when they will become conscious of their strength and become aware of the continuous injustice they suffer under Ingsoc.

At one point Winston tries to have a conversation with an old prole in a pub, buying him a drink to try to get him to talk. Winston wants to hear about his obsession, the past, what things were like once. He wants to see if anything has survived in the old man's memory, as, being a prole, he would know nothing of the techniques of doublethink. He asks him about the capitalists, which, according to Party history books, owned everything before the Revolution, but the old man can tell him nothing of any substance. His mind is a 'rubbish-heap of details' (p.77), a jumble of personal reminiscence.

And yet Winston retains his ideals about the proles. For him they stand as a symbol for the warmth of humanity; to him it seems as if they have not as yet severed the natural human ties of kinship and fellow-feeling, ties which he partly recovers in his affair with Julia.

In a backyard under the window of the room Winston and Julia rent, 'a monstrous woman, solid as a Norman pillar, with brawny red forearms and a sacking apron strapped about her middle' (p.113), seems to be always hanging out washing, singing as she does. She becomes, for Winston, a symbol of natural vitality, a humanity that will, in the end, strike back:

> Sooner or later it would happen, strength would change into consciousness. The proles were immortal, you could not doubt it when you looked at that valiant figure in the yard. . . . The birds sang, the proles sang, the Party did not sing. All round the world . . . stood the same solid unconquerable figure, made monstrous by work and child-bearing, toiling from birth to death and still singing. Out of those mighty loins a race of conscious beings must one day come. You were the dead; theirs was the future. But you could share in that future if you kept alive the mind as they kept alive the body, and passed on the secret doctrine that two plus two make four. (pp.175-6)

The proles sing like the thrush in the wood. They have a natural connection with life, whereas the Party is a denial of life. They are in touch with 'the process of life',* whereas the Party puts microphones among the leaves. The passage above fully states the true socialism of Winston, a socialism that has nothing in common with the distortion of it that is Ingsoc. Some day, Winston feels, the real revolution will take place; some day there will be peace on earth. He sees this potential in the proles. The last section of the novel acts as a powerful negative comment on this idealism. We should not be too quick to infer that this passage about the proles contains the essence of Orwell's own socialist idealism. It may be that Orwell did, to some extent, believe something like this – that Man's hope lay in the great suppressed humanity of ordinary people – but the last one third of the book which takes place in the torture chambers of the Ministry of Love explores Man's boundless capacity for cruelty and intolerance. The book sets the humanist, socialist optimism of Winston Smith against the pessimism of despair, and it is the latter that wins.

The 'valiant' washerwoman in the yard is a symbol of pathetic, moving, but finally unconvincing, hope.

*The phrase is from Orwell's essay 'Lear, Tolstoy and the Fool', *Inside the Whale*, pp.116–17; 'Shakespeare . . . loved the surface of the earth and the process of life'.

Language

Good prose, Orwell thought, should be like a window pane. It should allow the reader to see clearly for himself what the author has in mind. Clarity, for Orwell, was not just a virtue of the intellect: it was a moral virtue as well. The writer should be clear about what he thinks, and the language he uses to express himself should be simple, direct and plain: If a writer does not keep a clear conscience about the meaning of what he writes, the tired language of the day, with its vagueness, inactivity and laziness will take him over. In this lies the connection Orwell saw between language and politics. If a writer does not strive very hard to make his meaning clear, then his judgement and the judging quality of his language will become blurred. Totalitarianism, the great modern political threat, as Orwell saw it, thrives on the blurring of judgement, on vagueness of thought, of feeling, and most of all, of language. Indeed, if totalitarianism is to work at all, it needs to be able to get people to change their minds at will. It is easier to change one's mind if language (and thought, which Orwell saw as preceding language) is vague and indistinct.

It will be clear that Orwell is mainly concerned with prose style, and indeed poetry, with its necessary range of suggestion, implication, sometimes even vagueness, always made him slightly uneasy. The problems of the time were so acute that they needed the fine cutting edge of a simple, intelligent prose style to deal with them.

The language of *Nineteen Eighty-Four* is, on the whole, simple, direct and concrete. It presents the details of life in England in 1984 with great exactness and a careful attention to telling detail, so that the imagined world of the novel is given a sensuous reality, as in, for instance, the lengthy description of the sordid canteen in the Ministry of Love, or in the way Orwell has Winston notice how one could always tell Parsons had been playing table-tennis 'by the dampness of the bat handle' (p.48). Here Orwell is taking the trouble, as any good novelist must, to make his imagined world as concrete as possible, by finding appropriate images and the language in which to express them. But this imaginative quality in Orwell serves his political purpose: to show what day-to-day life might be like in a totalitarian state.

Orwell uses other kinds of language as well as this plain, direct style. In the sections which describe the meetings between Winston and Julia, he allows himself the luxury of a more poetic style, especially in passages connected with the paperweight or with the proles. Here is a passage describing the 'valiant' prole washerwoman:

> The mystical reverence that he felt for her was somehow mixed up with the aspect of the pale, cloudless sky, stretching away behind the chimney-pots into interminable distance. (p.175)

The reader should think about this passage. Does it work? Is it a bit too flowery? Is there a possibility that Orwell is being ironic here about Winston's idealistic tendencies, in view of what is to come?

Orwell also uses the dry language of political theory in the book within a book: *The Theory and Practice of Oligarchical Collectivism* by Emmanuel Goldstein. The language here is that of abstract, scientific analysis, clear but lacking in concreteness. This is appropriate for a book which is supposed to be an analysis of the Party's power.

Orwell also attempts to create an impression of the speech of the proles, based on London cockney. It is a dismal failure. See, for example, the exchange between Winston and the fat prole woman thrown in on top of him in the first of his cells in the Ministry of Love on p.183.

Apart from the different kinds of language Orwell uses in *Nineteen Eighty-Four,* language itself is one of the book's main themes. The society of 1984 is the society of Newspeak, the language of Ingsoc. Newspeak is still in the process of being invented, and as Syme the philologist points out to Winston, 'The Revolution will be complete when the language is perfect. Newspeak is Ingsoc and Ingsoc is Newspeak'.

This will be because the construction of Newspeak involves the wholesale destruction of English, Oldspeak, as it is called. In doing away with the words for *freedom, democracy, honour, justice, religion,* the theorists of Newspeak believe, these ideas themselves will disappear. And, if such ideas are gone, then thoughtcrime, the thinking of a thought critical of Party orthodoxy, will be impossible. Distinctions between shades of meaning, between good and evil, the basic judging ability of the free intelligence, will be no more, because the words will not be there for such unnecessary and dangerous refinements. Syme explains that in the end 'the whole notion of goodness and badness will be covered by only six words – in reality, only one word: 'ungood' = bad, 'plusgood' = very good, and so on (pp.44–5). Syme also points out that Winston is still drawn to the beauty of distinction and discrimination; he does not appreciate 'the beauty of the destruction of words'.

To be human is to discriminate and judge, and discrimination and judgement involve the exact use of language, so that the mind can know where it stands. Language and morality are closely related for Orwell. Not to use language clearly involves a descent to a kind of sub-human state, like the man sitting to Winston's left in the canteen, whose speech is just a 'noise uttered in unconsciousness', duckspeak, as it is called in Newspeak:

His head was thrown back a little, and because of the angle at which he was sitting, his spectacles caught the light and presented to

Winston two blank discs instead of eyes. What was slightly horrible, was that from the stream of sound that poured out of his mouth it was almost impossible to distinguish a single word. (p.46)

In an essay written in 1946, 'Politics and the English Language', Orwell had used this image of the two blank discs for eyes, in a description of a tired political hack on a platform, mouthing, like some mechanised dummy, strings of phrases which have nothing to do with thought, or with the process of human life:

One often has a curious feeling that one is not watching a live human being but some kind of dummy: a feeling which suddenly becomes stronger at moments when the light catches the speaker's spectacles and turns them into blank discs which seem to have no eyes behind them.*

The Appendix to the novel is an analysis of the main points about Newspeak. It is written in the past tense ('Newspeak was the official language of Oceania'), which may or may not indicate that the Party was overthrown at some stage, before the history of Winston Smith was written.

*Inside the Whale, p.152.

Part 4

Hints for study

IT IS WELL TO BEAR IN MIND that in most works of literature the author will have an overriding concern with certain themes, issues, or ideas. You cannot adequately describe these as the author's 'message' though that is a word often used, loosely, to describe a writer's central concerns. They go deeper than this, and have to do with the way he sees life, what his hopes are, what his fears, and what he thinks may be man's potential. In studying literary texts for examinations you should always try to decide what a writer's main preoccupations are, how they affect the work in question, and how successful he is in conveying to you, the reader, the urgency that made him write about them. If you can decide what the main preoccupations of a given work of literature are, you will have a centre from which you may proceed, with a sense of assurance, to examine other aspects.

What are Orwell's main concerns in *Nineteen Eighty-Four*? What are those things for which he wished 'to get a hearing'? In the essay 'Why I Write' Orwell tells us that 'every line of serious work' he has written since 1936 was against 'totalitarianism', and by totalitarianism he means the kind of state system, whether right or left wing, which tries to deny the individual's right to freedom of thought and expression. Orwell's central concern is always the asserting of the right of the individual intelligence to see, assess, and, finally, to judge for itself. *Nineteen Eighty-Four* is Orwell's final exploration of this concern of his; it lies behind every aspect of the novel, from its purpose to its structure.

In almost any question on *Nineteen Eighty-Four* you will find yourself writing about the novel's overriding concern, its main *theme:* the preciousness of human freedom, and its fragility. This main theme is part of Orwell's *purpose* as a writer, and in studying his purpose (see the section on purpose in the Commentary) you should look up, read, and use, the essays by Orwell quoted in these notes.

The main theme, then, and the purpose, are closely linked. There are many other themes radiating out from the main theme. Some of these are: love, hate, guilt, the past, and so on. It will be obvious that you cannot begin to consider these, and indeed the main theme itself, in isolation. A theme in a successful work of literature is not something that can be lifted out and looked at separately; if the writer has satisfactorily knitted up his *structure* the theme will involve discussion of other aspects, and especially, in the case of a novel or play, of *character* and *symbolism*. Character is the means by which a novelist explores his themes; symbolism the means by which he focuses on certain aspects of them from time to time.

For example, through Winston and Julia, Orwell explores the themes of human freedom, love, guilt and the past; through Winston and O'Brien he explores the themes of hate, guilt, and cruelty. Through the symbol of the paperweight, the tiny crinkle of coral inside its soft glass, he focuses on the precious and fragile world of feeling that Winston and Julia possess; through the symbol of Winston's ulcer he focuses upon, first, the healing influences of love and self-knowledge, and then, later, in the Ministry of Love, Winston's hopeless and inevitable degradation.

This novel has, like many Shakespearean tragedies, two main points of *climax*. (There is an appropriateness in the comparison with Shakespearean tragedy. Why? For further information on this see the discussion of Winston's character.) The first of these occurs when Winston and Julia are looking down from the window of their room at the prole woman hanging out washing. 'We are the dead', they say, and the telescreen hidden behind the old engraving of the church repeats the phrase in an 'iron voice'. The Thought Police thunder in and one of them smashes the paperweight. Read this scene very closely. The two worlds of the novel, the private one of Julia and Winston, the public one of the Party, collide at this point. The scene is full of loud crashing, breaking, smashing, shouting, and lastly, physical violence.

The other climax comes, of course, in Room 101. Here we have the final betrayal of the private world broken up so viciously in the first climax: Winston wants them to put the rats to Julia's face rather than his, just as one of the men in the cells earlier on had screamed for his children to be taken to Room 101 rather than himself. This climax suggests the end of all human self-respect and value.

The grey *atmosphere* of this novel, based on Orwell's experiences of war-time and post-war London, contributes to its main theme, the hopelessness of human life without the freedom to think or to love. Orwell goes to great trouble to be exact about the miserable details of life in his imagined world: sinks clogged with human hair; grease on everything in the canteen; slop everywhere; socks sticky for lack of washing. All this gives the novel a compulsive, sordid realism. This contributes to his purpose too: Orwell wants us to be sickened by the texture of life which, he fears, might exist under English socialism.

There is, of course, a conflict between Winston and the state. Orwell explores this in his development of Winston's character.

Useful quotations

The quotations given in the commentary, and their context in the text itself, should be studied carefully. Some others which may prove useful are given here.

(1) 'The hallway smelt of boiled cabbage and old rag mats.' (p.5)

This sets the atmosphere immediately.

(2) 'How do we know that two and two make four? Or that the force of gravity works? Or that the past is unchangeable? If both the past and the external world exist only in the mind, and if the mind itself is controllable – what then?' (p.68)

Winston doubts himself. Maybe the Party is right. Maybe everything is subjective and there is no objective reality.

(3) 'He was standing in front of a wall of darkness, and on the other side of it there was something unendurable, something too dreadful to be faced. In the dream his deepest feeling was always one of self-deception, because he did in fact know what was behind the wall of darkness. With a deadly effort, like wrenching a piece out of his own brain, he could even have dragged the thing into the open. He always woke up without discovering what it was'. (pp. 118–19)

This is a recurring dream of Winston's about a sub-conscious and unknown horror. Only in Room 101 does he find out what that horror behind the wall is, and then O'Brien uses it to get him to betray Julia. It is Winston's irrational fear of rats, and though he is not fully aware of it, the Party is.

(4) 'Even in using the word *doublethink* it is necessary to exercise *doublethink*. For by using the word one admits that one is tampering with reality; by a fresh act of *doublethink* one erases this knowledge: and so indefinitely, with the lie always one leap ahead of the truth. Ultimately it is by means of *doublethink* that the Party has been able . . . to arrest the course of history.' (p.171)

This is an extract from *The Book* of Emmanuel Goldstein, and is a clear and concise analysis of the process of doublethink, or reality control, so necessary in maintaining the stability of the Party.

(5) 'We make the laws of Nature.' (p.213)

O'Brien says this during Winston's 'reintegration'. Here O'Brien asserts the ultimate authority of the Party, that there is no truth of the senses, that the Party controls all truth, even gravity. If O'Brien believes he can float and Winston believes in O'Brien's belief, then, perhaps O'Brien may indeed, in some sense, float. This kind of thinking is entirely opposed to Winston's on p.68: 'Stones are hard, water is wet, objects unsupported fall to the earth's centre.' The freedom to believe this is the basic freedom: two plus two make four. All else follows that.

Answering questions

Always remember when answering questions in examinations to read the question very carefully and to satisfy yourself that you have fully understood what is required of you. Then plan your answer, making a list of points you wish to cover. You should then decide on the order in which you would cover them: you should aim for your ideas to flow smoothly one into the other, without blurring or confusing them.

When answering questions on *Nineteen Eighty-Four* you should bear the following points in mind:

(1) In answering a question on *character* or *characterisation* you will find yourself mainly dealing with Winston, but do not forget to mention Julia, O'Brien and some of the minor characters as well: Syme, Parsons, the prole woman – even, perhaps, Parsons' children.

(2) In answering a question on the main themes of the novel you should indicate these (freedom, love, hate, guilt, cruelty etc.), and show how they reveal Orwell's main purpose: to warn of the dangers he saw in the political tendencies of his time. You could then go on to point out that Orwell achieves this purpose by showing these themes at work in the development of Winston's character.

(3) In a question like 'Is *Nineteen Eighty-Four* more a work of political propaganda than a work of literary excellence?' you could consider the relationship between politics and writing for Orwell. You could also consider possible weaknesses in the novel. Is the last section overlong? Does Orwell prolong the agony too much, seeing that there are really only two characters worth speaking of in the last section? Is the climax in Room 101 a bit melodramatic? Is the book as a whole too pessimistic? These are questions which the reader should decide upon for himself.

(4) In a general question like 'Discuss the effectiveness of *Nineteen Eighty-Four*', you could possibly bring in his use of the conventions of the scientific romance.

Some questions and answers

Orwell once wrote: 'I see that it is invariably where I lacked a *political* purpose that I wrote lifeless books'. Does Orwell bring his political and his artistic concerns together in *Nineteen Eighty-Four*?

Orwell once said that his writing almost always began with a sense of injustice, of there being something wrong, either in society or in human nature, that needed to be put right. Writing was the means of exposing the wrong, of showing it to be humanly unacceptable. It will be clear, then, that Orwell regarded the writer as someone who should value and protect human freedom, and that it is up to him, because of his gift of language, to expose anyone or anything that would infringe upon that freedom.

The period when Orwell was writing his major works, from about 1936 up to his death in 1950, was the period which saw the rise of totalitarianism, especially in Nazi Germany. But, to Orwell, the problem was not confined there: he saw totalitarianism (the system of government where the rights of the state totally outweigh the rights of the individual) as being the major political tendency of the time. Because of this he felt the writer's job to be an urgent one in modern society. He should take care to understand the political make-up of the modern world, make his prose clear and effective, and use the forms that will best enable him to get a hearing.

Nineteen Eighty-Four is Orwell's warning against totalitarianism, but it is far from being merely a work of political propaganda. It is also a well-constructed novel in the tradition of the scientific romance. It mattered greatly to Orwell that he should get a hearing and that the urgency of the matter he was dealing with should be understood. So, instead of writing a theoretical analysis of the dangers of totalitarian government, whether of the right- or left-wing variety, he wrote a novel, which allowed him, through the atmosphere, and chiefly through the development of his main character, Winston Smith, to explore the inhuman reality of a life totally under government control. The form of novel he chose to write was the scientific romance.

The scientific romance is a recognised form of modern fiction, with a well-known set of conventions. These may be summarised briefly as follows: the action takes place sometime in the future, in a strange society; a main character is introduced to this society, learns its ways, and, very often, falls in love. The future society the writer imagines is often a way of commenting on present trends of which he disapproves, and the reader can usually share the sense of values of the main character. Now Orwell has, very carefully, adapted these conventions to his own political purposes. The society he imagines in *Nineteen Eighty-Four* is brutally remote from normal human values, and yet, for readers in the early 1950s, the London of the novel would not have been very different from the London of their own day. They would recognise the similarities and this would only serve to make the brutal political system of the novel all the more immediate.

It was a good idea to set the novel only thirty-six years ahead of the year in which it was written. It made people consider the world of *Nineteen Eighty-Four* as a real possibility. Was there a chance that the world they thought they knew so well could alter so much?

Winston Smith is, by the reader's standard, fairly normal in his assumptions about the value of human life and love. But by the standards of *Nineteen Eighty-Four* he is abnormal. At one stage in the novel, when the Ministry of Plenty announces that the chocolate ration has been *raised* to 20 grammes, when only the day before it had been announced that it was *reduced* to 20 grammes, he wonders if he is the only one with a memory. He is our representative in the novel, a representative of normal, feeling humanity, and through him that humanity is tested against the coldness of the Party's system.

Orwell has us share in, and sympathise with, Winston's growing self-realisation, his increasing affection for Julia. He has him arrive at an understanding of the power of love (it heals his ulcer), and of his own guilt (he remembers stealing his sister's chocolate). This understanding gives him dignity and consistency. It gives him strength. Then all this is shattered (symbolised in the shattering of the paperweight) when the Thought Police crash into the room over the junk shop where he and Julia spend their hours together. In the Ministry of Love his mind is washed clean of all thoughtcrime and he is made 'perfect' (as O'Brien once said he would be).

In getting us to sympathise with Winston's tragic fall from dignity Orwell is getting us to realise, not just understand, the human cost of a brutal political system. In this way the novelist and the political thinker come together in *Nineteen Eighty-Four*.

Examine Winston Smith's obsession with the past in *Nineteen Eighty-Four*.

Julia, the girl with whom Winston Smith falls in love, cannot understand why he is so preoccupied with the past. She is inclined to live for the moment and to let the future take care of itself. But as O'Brien makes Winston repeat in the torture chambers of the Ministry of Love: 'Who controls the past controls the future: who controls the present controls the past.' The Party depends for its survival on the control of the past. There must be absolute and total submission to the Party, therefore it cannot allow any memory of things other than those of which it approves. As the Party's policy is constantly changing (it switches from being at war with Eurasia to being at war with Eastasia every few years), and as its policy is that it never changes, it needs to have complete control over people's memories. Existing records are constantly being re-written to fit in with new developments; that is the function of the Ministry of Truth: to make history one huge, shifting lie.

Any problems individuals might have in their minds, in altering their memories of past events to fit in with the new information, are dealt with by the technique of doublethink, the ability to know something is the case, and yet, at the same time, know it is not the case.

Winston is not perfectly orthodox. The continual altering of the past, to fit in with new developments, which he himself is very good at, disturbs him deeply. Doublethink disgusts him. He is drawn, imaginatively, to the past. He buys a diary in an old junk shop in a prole quarter of London. The diary attracts him because of its old-fashioned creamy paper. In it he wants to make a kind of personal history that will be true, that will connect him as he is living now to how he was when he was living in the past. In other words he is a man in search of continuity, of identity. In this he is like many heroes of modern fiction, from Meursault in *The Outsider* (1942) by Albert Camus (1913–60) to Yossarian in *Catch 22* (1961) by Joseph Heller (*b*.1923), the American novelist. He seeks continuity with the past because he knows he cannot be fully human until he remembers and understands himself.

The Party gets rid of unwanted records by sending the papers down the memory holes. For the Party there is no such thing as a fixed record, that is, there is no such thing as objective truth. The Party *is* the Truth; individual memory of different truth is not just insignificant – it is a crime. Winston's quest, in the novel, is to find *his* truth, and this can only be done by understanding his past. He seeks individual self-knowledge, where the Party would have him believe that the individual does not matter. He seeks clarity, understanding, and this comes through love, his love for Julia. Love restores him, and it restores his memory. He remembers, in a dream, his mother's love for his tiny starving sister, when he grabbed her share of a precious slab of chocolate. He remembers the way in which she put her arm around the little girl in a protective gesture, and this enfolding of the arm connects, in his mind, with the gesture he saw a woman make in a film, when she tried, vainly, to protect a little boy from a hail of bullets. This circular gesture also connects with the soft roundness of the paperweight (itself 'a chunk of history' the Party has left unaltered) inside of which the dream of recollection takes place. The coral at the heart of the rainwater softness of the paperweight stands, in the novel, for the love between Winston and Julia.

The past, regained through love, was a time when there was in society in general, and not just between exceptional individuals, a code of loyalty and kinship. This gave dignity to life, a tragic dignity. Now there is only pain, fear, and heartlessness. The past, in Winston's mind, is associated with his dream of the Golden Country, a beautiful country landscape in which life was sane and whole. When he dreams of it he wakes with the word 'Shakespeare' on his lips. For a brief time Winston gains a Shakespearean dignity, through Julia, when the love he lost once comes back, only to lose it all over again, hopelessly, in the Ministry of Love.

Discuss the relationship between Winston Smith and O'Brien in *Nineteen Eighty-Four*.

Winston Smith works in the Ministry of Truth, altering the past, telling the lies necessary for the Party to survive. O'Brien is an Inner Party member, but Winston feels, instinctively, that there is some kind of secret understanding between them. He had a dream, once, some seven years before the action of the novel begins, in which he is in a pitch dark room and a voice which he always associated with O'Brien says: 'We shall meet in the place where there is no darkness'. By the end of the novel we know that this place is the Ministry of Love, with its harsh, ever-burning electric lights.

Winston admires O'Brien; he has a heavy, almost a prize-fighter's, physique, but he has a curiously elegant, almost old-fashioned way of settling his spectacles on his nose. Eventually O'Brien mentions a man called Syme to Winston, and, Syme being an unperson, that is, someone vaporised by the Party, and so a forbidden topic of conversation, Winston interprets this as an invitation to participate in conspiracy. He believes O'Brien to be a member of the Brotherhood, a secret organisation, supposedly dedicated to the overthrow of Big Brother. He visits O'Brien's flat where he and Julia are sworn into the Brotherhood. But it is all an elaborate trap. O'Brien is not just an Inner Party member, he is one of the directors of torture in the Ministry of Love, where Winston and Julia are then taken.

In the last section of the book the strangeness in the relationship between Winston and O'Brien emerges. They are virtually the only characters in this part of the book, torturer and victim. Oddly, Winston still feels a very strong sense of attachment to O'Brien; he even has feelings of love towards him, as he leans over him, with his strong ugly face.

But why this feeling of love that Winston has for him? It is not fully explained, but there is, possibly, in Winston, a sense of relief that the deception is over, a gratefulness that he has, at last, come to face his fate at O'Brien's hands, which he always knew to be there, awaiting him. Further, it may be that Winston, feeling guilty about the early betrayal of his mother's love and his cruelty towards his sister, welcomes punishment, to burn out the memory. It may be that, after all, Winston does not want the responsibility of being an individual, of holding on to his own version of the truth in spite of the Party's insistence on its truth. It is easier to give in to the larger mind of the Party, embodied in O'Brien's mind, which, Orwell says, 'contained' Winston's.

Part 5

Suggestions for further reading

The text

ORWELL, GEORGE: *Nineteen Eighty-Four,* Martin Secker & Warburg, London, 1949; Penguin Books, Harmondsworth, 1975. The later of two 1975 editions is cited in these notes.

Other works by the author

ORWELL, GEORGE: *Inside the Whale and Other Essays,* first published as *Selected Essays,* Penguin Books, Harmondsworth, 1957; Penguin Books, Harmondsworth, 1976. This edition is referred to in these notes.

ORWELL, GEORGE: *The Collected Essays, Journalism and Letters,* Martin Secker & Warburg, London, 1968; Penguin Books, Harmondsworth, 1971. This edition is referred to in these notes.

ORWELL, GEORGE: *The Road to Wigan Pier,* Victor Gollancz, London, 1937; Penguin Books, Harmondsworth, 1971. This edition is referred to in these notes.

General reading

ALLDRITT, KEITH: *The Making of George Orwell,* Edward Arnold, London, 1969. This is useful in studying both Orwell's relationship with the symbolist movement, and his handling of the scientific romance.

MACKENZIE, NORMAN AND JEANNE: *The Time Traveller: The Life of H.G. Wells,* Weidenfeld & Nicolson, London, 1973. This gives detailed information on Wells's scientific romances.

SANDISON, ALAN: *The Last Man in Europe,* Macmillan, London, 1974. This places Orwell in the English radical Protestant tradition, and deals with the mysterious bond between Winston and O'Brien.

THOMAS, EDWARD M.: *Orwell,* Oliver & Boyd, Edinburgh and London, 1965. This is good on the theme of power in the novel, and on Orwell's moral attitudes.

WILLIAMS, RAYMOND (ED.): *George Orwell: A Collection of Critical Essays,* Prentice-Hall, Englewood Cliffs, New Jersey, 1974. Isaac Deutscher's essay attacks *Nineteen Eighty-Four* because of its despair; Conor Cruise O'Brien, in his essay, finds Orwell somewhat provincial in his Englishness, but admires him for his moral anger.

WILLIAMS, RAYMOND: *Orwell,* Fontana/Collins, Glasgow, 1971. This is interesting on Orwell's politics and critical of the vision of *Nineteen Eighty-Four.*

The author of these notes

ROBERT WELCH is a graduate of University College, Cork, and of the University of Leeds. He was a lecturer at the University of Ife, Nigeria, before taking up a post as Lecturer in English at the University of Leeds. He is now Professor of English and Head of Department at the University of Ulster at Coleraine, Northern Ireland. He has written on English and Anglo-Irish literature, including a *Companion to Anglo-Irish Literature*. He is also the author of the York Notes on Edmund Spenser's *The Faerie Queene* (Book I) and George Orwell's *Animal Farm*.

York Handbooks: list of titles

YORK HANDBOOKS form a companion series to York Notes and are designed to meet the wider needs of students of English and related fields. Each volume is a compact study of a given subject area, written by an authority with experience in communicating the essential ideas to students of all levels.

AN INTRODUCTORY GUIDE TO ENGLISH LITERATURE
by MARTIN STEPHEN

PREPARING FOR EXAMINATIONS IN ENGLISH LITERATURE
by NEIL McEWAN

EFFECTIVE STUDYING
by STEVE ROBERTSON *and* DAVID SMITH

THE ENGLISH NOVEL
by IAN MILLIGAN

ENGLISH POETRY
by CLIVE T. PROBYN

DRAMA: PLAYS, THEATRE AND PERFORMANCE
by MARGERY MORGAN

AN INTRODUCTION TO LINGUISTICS
by LORETO TODD

STUDYING CHAUCER
by ELISABETH BREWER

STUDYING SHAKESPEARE
by MARTIN STEPHEN *and* PHILIP FRANKS

AN A·B·C OF SHAKESPEARE
by P. C. BAYLEY

STUDYING MILTON
by GEOFFREY M. RIDDEN

STUDYING CHARLES DICKENS
by K. J. FIELDING

STUDYING THOMAS HARDY
by LANCE ST JOHN BUTLER

STUDYING THE BRONTËS
by SHEILA SULLIVAN

STUDYING JAMES JOYCE
by HARRY BLAMIRES

ENGLISH LITERATURE FROM THE THIRD WORLD
by TREVOR JAMES

ENGLISH USAGE
by COLIN G. HEY

ENGLISH GRAMMAR
by LORETO TODD

STYLE IN ENGLISH PROSE
by NEIL McEWAN

AN INTRODUCTION TO LITERARY CRITICISM
by RICHARD DUTTON

A DICTIONARY OF LITERARY TERMS
by MARTIN GRAY

READING THE SCREEN
An Introduction to Film Studies
by JOHN IZOD